The CURSED MONASTERY

A TALE OF CHARLES ISLAND

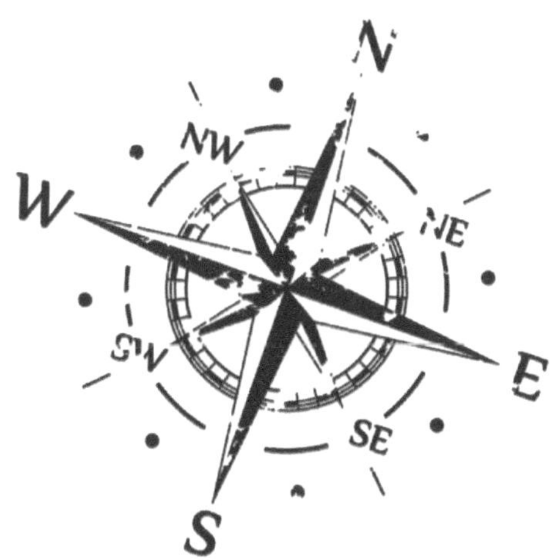

MARISSA D'ANGELO

Dedication

This book is dedicated to my Nonni Rose

You have shown me how to be strong through the most difficult obstacles that life can give. Thank you for teaching me to be a fighter and continue to believe no matter how hard it gets.

Books by Marissa D'Angelo

Tales of Charles Island Series

The Cursed Spirit

The Cursed Spirit 2

The Cursed Vessel

The Cursed Inn

The Cursed Monastery

Presence

Other Books

The Vanished

Chasing Time

Author's Note

Since the release of this book, I have wanted to find some way to help Charles Island and the wildlife that it supports. A local reforestation group is working hand in hand with the Connecticut Department of Energy and Environmental Protection to plant more trees so that the island and its wildlife can survive and thrive.

Message from Reforestation Group:

We want to restore the island to its former state. After years of invasive species and diseases, we need to help nature along with this task.

10% of the proceeds from this series will go to this cause.

The Beginning

1

In the beginning God created the heavens and the earth. And the earth was a formless and desolate emptiness, and darkness was over the surface of the deep, and the Spirit of God was hovering over the surface of the waters. Then God said, "Let there be light"; and there was light.

(Genesis 1:1-3)

After many stormy days, the sun finally emerged from behind the clouds. The brutal heat that came was unbearable as crowds flocked to the shores to cool off. I couldn't resist the urge to follow them. Even being in the lowest level of the house was exhausting. No work could be done on the farm once the sun soared high in the sky. It would force us to wake early to get any and all work done. The farm had been in the family for a while and it was how we made a living, but things fell apart when the war came. Everything seemed to fall apart.

 I felt my father's compass that he had left me clunk in my pocket as I walked into the kitchen. I treasured it most because it was the one thing that could always bring me back home, no matter how lost I was. I was somehow able to hold on to it throughout the war as, thankfully, we were not displaced, and it never left my side since. It had been a little under a year since the war ended and troops were pulled out of the thick of it. I remembered the day Father had left like it was yesterday. I thought about what he was doing out there every single second of the day. When schools closed and I had to help Mother on the farm, I would always keep an eye peeled so that I didn't miss him when he finally came home. The hope that he would someday come back never faded. I clasped my hand around the compass and felt its cold metallic case, thinking of the moments before it was even given to me.

"Lucy," he called outside when I was just thirteen years old, likely getting into trouble. I remembered I was supposed to be working and doing chores the whole time, so I thought I had been caught and would get yelled at upon my return. I made sure to saunter extra slowly, as I was in no rush to be punished.

The moment I walked closer into view of the house and the back steps, I could see the disappointment in my father's eyes, but it wasn't because of me. Several men in uniform stood behind him while Mother was on her knees, sobbing.

"Father, what is it?" I immediately asked and rushed up to him, eyeing the men in uniform.

"I need to go." He looked back at the men and they nodded as if they approved of what he had said to me.

"But where?"

"I have been summoned to war."

As soon as the last word left his mouth, Mother wailed like she had been pierced through the heart with a knife. I ran over to her and hugged her, not fully understanding at the time what this had meant for our family.

"It's okay, Mother. Father will be back. Right?" I looked over my shoulder at him and it seemed the men in uniform were rushing him in some way. He walked over to me slowly and got down to his knees, hugging Mother and me close to him. I felt Mother shaking uncontrollably and wished I could help her feel better. I had never seen her like this before.

"No matter what, we all end up together. Just remember that" he said.

When he got up and headed inside, I followed like a lost puppy dog would follow the only person who fed them. His bag had already been packed, and I immediately regretted taking so long outside and not coming in right away. It was time I would never get back with him. The men in the uniforms stood by the front door, waiting. He saluted them and asked if they could spare him a moment longer and that he would be right out. Both of them filed out, closing the door behind them. Father turned toward me and bent down so he could be more on my level and look me right in the eyes.

"Lucy, there is one lesson in life that you must know, and I am sorry you have to learn it at such a young age. There are things in life we cannot control; we must simply embrace the change and accept what is to come. While I am gone, you and your mother must look after one another.

I know you were out there avoiding your chores and that's okay. I wish you could be a child and do trouble-maker things for a bit longer, but this is the day you need to grow up and take responsibility for our family. Take care of your mother and remember, we will see each other again."

I could barely process everything he said but felt a tear stream down my cheek because he had known I was avoiding my chores all along, but he still cared for me and understood me. I pressed my head into his shoulder and let my tears pour out, soaking his shirt.

"Lucy." He pushed me away from him and pulled out a handkerchief, wiping my tears. "Hold out your hand."

I obeyed.

He placed something in my hand that was far too big for me to hold and gave me a shock as soon as it touched my skin. When he moved his hand away from it, I saw a compass that had four inscriptions on it:

north, south, east and west in cursive. The arrow pointed in between the North and East signs.

"You see this?" He pointed to where the arrow was, and I nodded my head. "This will make sure you are never lost. Do not ever part from it."

"Won't you need it?" I asked.

"Not where I'm going. And in any case, they will likely give us one if we do need direction. I want you to keep this on you so you never lose your way." He closed my fingers over the compass and wrapped his arm around me, hugging me one final time. He kissed me on the forehead and opened the door to leave.

I wanted to beg him to stay or hide him somewhere, so the men in uniform didn't have to take him away. Instead, I ran over to the window to watch as Father walked to the truck with his duffel bag over his shoulder. Mother ran from around back and he stopped and turned, opening up his arms wide to catch her. She practically threw herself onto him and he spun her around; her feet were fully off the ground. They kissed and hugged for so long that I barely noticed my breath fogging up the window that I pressed my face against, yearning to be out there too.

I picked my hand up and looked at the compass again, holding it close to my chest as if hugging it was like hugging Father. It was nowhere close, but it was something.

That day had been at least ten years ago, and I still clung to the compass just as I had when I was just a young girl. Having a reminder of who I was even when I had thought I lost myself completely kept me grounded. Something in me told me to use it that day and go wherever it took me. I wasn't exactly sure how, but I was desperate for answers.

Trust

2

When I made my way downstairs, Mother was in the kitchen washing dishes. She was there physically, except it didn't seem like her mind was, as she gazed out the window. I would often find her like this in the morning. Her long black hair reached down to her waist. After Father left, she had stopped caring about her looks. She no longer got dressed up or even left the house. If she needed something from town, I would go fetch it for her.

The kitchen table was completely clear except for a Bible that laid open beside the chair Mother usually sat at. I slowly walked over to it and peered at the passage it laid open to:

Proverbs 3:5-6 - Trust in the Lord with all your heart, and do not lean on your own understanding. In all your ways acknowledge him, and he will make straight your paths.

I had trusted in the Lord all along and it never brought Father back here no matter how long and hard I prayed each night. But somehow, he would straighten my path? My tangled web of a path that my life had become since Father left? All along, I had felt a weight on my shoulders and the work on the farm became so much that I couldn't even attend school any longer and had to drop out shortly after Father left. But somehow…Mother still believed the Lord would straighten our paths.

I looked over at her as she continued to wash dishes and felt sorry for her as she was barely hanging on to a string of hope and continued to confide in the Bible. I wished I could be more like her in a way, but instead, I was much more direct and impulsive like Father had been. Her morning routine was something I rarely wanted to interrupt because it was one of the few things that remained constant after Father left.

The compass clunked in my pocket, reminding me of him. I felt a push from behind me to go give her a hug. It nearly made me jump out of my skin. When I looked behind me, there was no one. I quickly shrugged it off and tried to head toward the door, hoping she didn't hear me.

"Hey Lucy." She seemed to know I was there this entire time. Her voice almost startled me, since she didn't even look back when she said my name.

"You must have eyes on the back of your head," I admitted. She was more attuned to her surroundings than me.

"Where are you headed?" she asked, looking down at my pocket, knowing full well I always kept the compass in there.

"I just want to go walk for a bit," I said, realizing how easy it must have been to see right through me. Any emotion I felt, no matter what, she would always recognize right away. I could try to bury it or mask how I felt, but there would never be a day when it would work on her.

She walked toward me as she dried her hands with a towel. They were still wet as she grasped my wrist.

"You are grown now, and I know your father made you promise to be the lady of the house and take care of the farm, but you need to also remember what is in here." She pressed her hand to my chest. "Your father and I had our chance at life, and we created a beautiful one. It is your turn now, Lu."

"I won't be gone long," I said, remembering Father had said something quite similar. I would be different from him, though. I would keep my promise.

"Maybe you will meet a guy when you go and you can finally have some children that can do some of the work on the farm here," she changed the subject.

"Keep wishing, but don't hold your breath!" I laughed and felt my spirits lifted at her joke. It was bittersweet because there was a time when there could have been someone in my life, but the war was quick to change everything.

I gave her a hug, and she packed some bread for me to bring out on my journey. I took out the compass and smiled, ready to face something I never thought I would.

The Island

3

Father spoke of an island that seemed as if it were made up. I always wanted to go there since I was little, because his stories intrigued me. He would say that at a certain time each day, the water would retreat and reveal a pathway to an island that many would steer clear of due to the history of rumors and deaths surrounding it. People still ventured out there, though. It puzzled me as to what made him continuously go out there to the island despite the risks. I yearned to see exactly what my father saw before he went out to war. I thought about what he may have had to endure when he was drafted, along with hundreds of other men.

The dirt roads quickly turned into a grassy area and, as the salty sea filled the air, my heart only yearned for more. I could hear the waves crash against the shore, but still saw nothing. A long wall of bushes lined the area where the sand began. It made me think of the trenches that Father hid within, likely holding on to the string of hope that would bring him back home to his family again. I knew I had to go south in order to find the island. When I looked at my compass, that was the direction I had been going all along. For a while, there was nothing. I continued on, growing impatient. The farther I went, the more I clung to the compass in my pocket as if I were already lost. Just when I was about to turn around, a clearing between the bushes appeared. It was as if it were the perfect doorway to something on the other side I couldn't have imagined in my wildest dreams. It was a wonder how the bushes and trees didn't grow in this one place, but they did everywhere else. I paused and felt torn. It was almost as if something was pulling me back from continuing on, but at the same time, there was an opposing push. I went with the latter.

I immediately felt myself sink into the sand a bit with each step forward. When I finally walked through the opening, the coast was lined with sandy shores and past the water was the island. A thick cloud floated above it and from here, it seemed that it was a great distance away, definitely unreachable by foot. I continued walking through the sand, looking to my left and right to find no one. It was still early in the morning, so I had time to explore without anyone near. I almost continued walking through the water because I couldn't tear my eyes off the island. Mesmerized with wonder, I stared out and felt goosebumps spread up my arms. It was overwhelmingly hot, but I felt chills the longer I looked out. Trees towered on the island, almost making it appear to be a giant bush. From the stories, I questioned how there could have been an inn there, or anything else for that matter, within such a thick forest of trees. I walked along the coast, thinking up hundreds of questions that would likely go unanswered.

The sand stretched out toward the island, forming a perfect pathway to go right to it. The compass felt even heavier in my pocket. If anything was a sign to not go out there, this was it. I couldn't help my curiosity, though. I wondered if there were any remnants on the island and if so, what were they?

A strong breeze passed through, and I folded my arms over my chest, cold for some reason despite the heat of the summer. As I neared the edge of the shore and the beginning of the path that led straight to the island, I could see the faint outline of another person. They were looking out toward me. My hesitation to walk there quickly faded. Instead, I was pulled there and any warning to stay back was pushed to the back of my mind. He was staring right back at me and looked as though he needed my help. The sandy pathway changed to a rocky, shell-covered path. I could feel the soles of my shoes crunch with each step I took. When I was just halfway there, water pooled in my shoes and I realized the tide was coming in, washing up the path that would bring me to him. When I backed up a little to get out of the water, I looked out at the island again to find he was gone. It was as if there was no one even there to begin with. I brought out my compass; although I was definitely facing the south, the arrow pointed directly at me. I gave it a shake, and it stayed exactly where it was.

"He will make straight your paths," I said the last part of the proverbs that I had read from Mother's Bible aloud. I felt like the path that lay before me and lead straight to the island was enough to show me that this is where I was meant to be. Part of me wanted to continue on and didn't care about getting soaked from the tide that was just coming in. I could just take off my shoes and place them on the shore and swim out to the island. But how would I get back? I thought of the many lives lost out here and realized how the island could lure one's soul so they couldn't turn back. Time was not on my side. The waves pushed in, covering more and more of the pathway. I decided to turn around. If he were truly there, I would find him again. It could have been that I was growing slightly delusional...in which case, I would surely end up in a madhouse.

I decided not to tell a soul.

Warning

4

If only I had known that would have just been the first of many strange occurrences, I would've never walked out to the island like I had. But there was no avoiding its inescapable pull as it overwhelmed and had a way of taking over any control I thought I had.

"Lucy, wait up!" a hoarse voice called out to me. I turned around to find James coming toward me.

James was an old friend from the schooldays. Both of our fathers had gone out together in the war, but his came back unlike mine. I had a lingering hope my father was still out there. He quickly became like a little brother to me. He was always following me around and seeking me out to give him advice about some lady friends. When his father went to war, he was much younger than I had been. He likely barely even remembered him much, but I looked after him as much as I could until his father came back. The day that his father came back, I remember I was so sure mine would be following closely behind. James ran up to him, and I'll never forget the look on his father's face. His happiness from greeting his family and finally seeing them again instantly turned to a sullen darkness as the grim look spread over his face when he locked eyes with me. He shook his head slowly so as to let me know my father was not with him and would not be coming back.

"What are you doing here? Following?" I asked, spooked and wondering how much he saw. Did he see the man like I had?

"I was wondering the exact same about you, but maybe we're both here for the same reason."

"Which is…?" I asked, trying not to give more away than I already had just by being there.

"You didn't hear?" The wind blew his dirty-blond hair over to the other side. It went down to about his chin. He was a little taller than me and had a stocky stature.

"Okay, just get to it, James."

"You know that old inn that was on the island in the latter part of the 1800s? Well, they've decided to build a religious retreat there." He stood proud with a hand on each of his sides. News that he got to before I had even heard.

"Why on earth would they do that?" I asked, remembering the stories.

"Well, you know…" He gestured behind him in the direction of the island.

"They think sprinkling some holy water on that damned land is going to do it justice? Well, good luck," I called out over my shoulder and continued walking back home. I could hear him scurry after me.

"You still haven't answered my question," he said.

"And that was…?"

"What were you doing out there?" He persisted.

"Can't I go for a nice walk?" I smiled, knowing he wouldn't believe it for a minute.

"Okay, whatever… so, our crew is putting together plans to head out there and we're going to help build the retreat. Starting tomorrow."

"That's not a good idea…"

"And why not?"

"You know."

"Well, I've got to make money somehow. There's no way I can just refuse; it'll cost me."

There was silence the rest of the way. The sun emerged from the clouds and beamed down on us. I instantly regretted not remembering to bring water along. I wanted to tell him what I saw, but felt like I already knew the response, as it sounded crazy enough in my own mind, let alone out loud.

"Is there anything you want to talk about? You seem off today…well, more off than you normally are."

"Thank you for that. I'm alright, I'll see you tomorrow." I walked toward my house and James went the opposite way. As I continued on, I glanced over my shoulder to find that he was still in view. Something was eerie about his mention of the retreat on the island. For some reason, I felt I needed to stop him from going out there in a boat.

"Hey James?" I called back, stopping to turn around. He stopped in his tracks and put his arms out as if to ask what I wanted without saying it.

"Don't go out there on that boat," I said. "Just don't. Trust me. Okay?" I shouted over his way, and he just shrugged his shoulders and turned around, walking farther and farther away from me.

I felt like I could only control so much just as I was unable to keep Father here. A boat ride to the island seemed like it should be fine, but something in me felt the need to warn him. I had done what I could and was glad to be back home again. I wished I could tell Mother about what I had seen, but knew she wouldn't have believed me either.

When I walked inside, I was glad to find Mother was outside picking some flowers from the garden. I ran upstairs and pulled out the compass, falling flat onto my bed.

I closed my eyes and tried to reimagine the man I saw. He was much older than me, and I could hardly make out what he was wearing. It almost seemed as if he was in a fog I couldn't see completely clearly through. I rubbed my hands on the compass. One thing that was alarming was that he had a bag he was holding. I thought of what James had said. Was it possible they were already doing construction on the island, and he was just one of the workers or perhaps one of the fathers who decided to build the religious retreat in the first place? But something was off about this man...

"That was quick, Lucy! Come down here and let's get ready for church," Mother yelled up.

"Can we pray from home?" I asked, already knowing full well what the answer would be.

"Lucy Ann!" I rolled out of bed and practically fell to the ground. When she used my middle name, I knew not to push her any further. And although I didn't want to go, I couldn't bear to let her go all alone and without me. I made a promise to Father, and that was to make sure Mother wasn't alone in her times of need.

"Coming!"

I ran over to quickly change into something else. The walk in the morning made my clothes disgusting, and I was ready to get out of them as soon as possible. The first thing that caught my eye was a short-sleeved, green dress adjourned in white polka dots. It went down below the knees but was very light in comparison to the other clothes I had. I grabbed the straw cloche hat off the top of my dresser. It had a beige ribbon wrapped around it with a bow in the back. There was no need to wear any jewelry of any sort, but I looked again at the necklaces I had, and the pearls stood out to me. They were left to me by Father for when I reached of age. I slipped them on as quickly as I could and reluctantly put on my white heels. When I looked in the mirror, I found my face was red with sunburn and it looked as though I had blush all over my cheeks or was embarrassed about something since they were rosy red. I looked at my eyes and wished that they were Father's that I was looking into. We had the same color eyes and whenever I looked in the mirror, I would pretend for just a moment he was still here. I gently played with the pearls around my neck and knew it would be the right choice because I would have something that Father had given me on my way to church. I grabbed a pair of white lace gloves and rushed downstairs just as Mother was calling after me.

"Lucy, we're going to be late!" Mother yelled up.

"Coming, coming!" I called downstairs and rushed out the door with Mother.

Pray

5

The morning sun blared down on us as we walked down the road to the church. Other townsfolk went the same way, and at that moment, we were all like cattle herded into the same place. This was the most wretched time of the week, but also a good time. It was now that Mother and I had to wear masks over our faces to act as if everything was okay even though our hearts were broken to pieces and longed for Father.

But it was the one place we felt closest to him. The one place we felt a glimmer of hope.

As we filed into our usual pew that we sat in every week, I kneeled and began praying until they started. It was then that I could talk to Father, but part of me still had hope he was out there somewhere and would come home any day.

Our Father, Who art in heaven, hallowed be Thy name; Thy kingdom come; Thy will be done on earth as it is in heaven. Give us this day our daily bread; and forgive us our trespasses as we forgive those who trespass against us; and lead us not into temptation, but deliver us from evil.

I opened the Bible and flipped through its pages as I would commonly do each time Mother and I waited for mass to begin. When I peeked over, Mother was on her knees, resting her head against her folded hands in prayer. The sight of her desperation to be with Father again made my heart sink further in my chest. I looked down at the Bible, hoping for some answers.

Romans (8:24–25)

For in hope we have been saved, but hope that is seen is not hope; for who hopes for what he already sees? But if we hope for what we do not see, through perseverance we wait eagerly for it.

I reread the same passage several times to try to make sense of it. And what I realized was that we don't hope for things that we can already see because that means that we already have them. We are saved when we have hope because even if we are just holding on by a string of mere faith, that at least means we can keep going in life. That small sliver of hope allows us to wake up each day with a light before us…and sometimes that light is far greater than we could have ever imagined. I set aside the Bible and kneeled, pressing my head into my hands just like Mother had.

Father, the redundancy of life without you is nothing I could ever get used to. I'm trying to make Mother happy and we still have the farm, but times have been quite difficult, and it has been hard to make ends meet. I'll do whatever it takes to keep the farm. I still have hope. Today, there was a man out on the island that you used to speak of. Why did you used to go out there, Father? Well…the silly townspeople have decided to go build a retreat out there. They must have heard the stories of the inn…and the tragedies that occurred there. Father, if you are up there, please watch over them. I do have a very bad feeling about it.

As soon as I got my last thought out, I could hear everyone standing up from the squeaky wooden pews. Everyone faced the priest as he walked past each row. Chorus chimed in and I felt like everyone in the church echoed the song except for me. Even Mother sang out as she normally had. When Father came to church with us, he'd purposely bellow out his deep voice in each song. It would make me laugh so hard that Mother would beg Father to take me out of church right away and give me a spanking. But little did she know we would just continue giggling outside of the church the entire time.

I snapped out of it and flipped the missal open to the page they would be reading from. Before I could flip through the pages to find where the priest was, a sudden breeze came through the room and the pages gently turned on their own. I looked up and everyone was frozen in a state of dormancy. I exhaled and saw my breath in front of me as if it were much colder than it had actually been. A tear that fell from Mother's eye gently streamed down her cheek, dropping onto the missal she held open on her lap. It dampened the pages, searing through several. She had no reaction, but continued staring forward at the priest. I looked at everyone else and they remained in the same statue-like state. *Was I dreaming?*

I looked back down at my book to find it open to a specific verse that suited the moment quite well:

Matthew (24:40-41)

Two men will be in the field, one will be taken and the other left. Two women will be grinding with a hand mill; one will be taken and the other left.

Was it true that there may be some people left behind? Death may take their bodies, but their souls remain here until the end of time?

When I looked back at the priest, I could see someone from several pews before us glancing back at me. He had dark, tanned skin that reminded me of the color of Mother's morning coffee when she added just a bit of cream in. I had never seen him before, nor had I attended school with him. His dark hair was slicked back smoothly and appeared wet, as if he had just bathed. He wore a dark gray vest and his white sleeves were rolled up to his elbows. He wasn't frozen as everyone else had been. When I caught his gaze, his emerald eyes took hold of me and I felt even if I wanted to, I wouldn't have been able to break eye contact no matter how hard I tried. He ripped his gaze away from me and faced forward. Something about him made me feel an instant connection with him.

Before I could continue reading, the pages flipped back to the original place I had been and the priest's voice continued to his homily.

"Did you see that?" I whispered to Mother.

"Shhh, see what?" she asked and faced forward again, as if to say she wasn't going to humor my questions. I sighed. There was nothing at all the priest said that I was taking in. I couldn't concentrate on anything else. I just kept re-opening the book, inspecting it to figure out how it even happened. If I told anyone, I would surely end up in an asylum of some sort. The man that I locked eyes with definitely saw what I had seen because he was the only one still moving, just like I had been.

"Stop," Mother whispered and took the book from me, piling her own on top of it. I put my hand in my pocket and fiddled with the heavy compass.

The priest prompted us all to stand, and we followed. I crossed my arms, irritated and having no interest or motivation to be here. I wanted to get to the bottom of what happened. Deep down, I felt a longing to go back to the island…as if going back there would make sense.

I looked over at Mother, and she just shook her head. I put both arms out and mouthed 'what?'

The priest announced it was time for communion and we kneeled until it was time to get up and receive the sacrament. I stood behind Mother and watched as the green-eyed man took his place in the line. He was farther up than me in another line adjacent to the one I was in. When he took communion, he turned and stared toward his seat instead of looking my way again. I felt my heart sink as I was hoping to feel that connection once more.

"The Body of Christ." The priest broke me out of my trance, and I almost jumped. When I opened my mouth, he placed the Eucharist on my tongue. I turned around to follow Mother back to our pew and pray, but made sure to look at the mystery man. When my eyes found his pew, there he was, kneeling and looking right up at me. His eyes pierced through my chest. The urgency in his stare made me feel a pull to come closer. I wanted to go back to kneel beside him, but instead, I followed

Mother into our pew, and we kneeled, praying until everyone had received communion.

"Thank you all for coming to worship with us today. We have a few announcements to make," the priest said before everyone. "One of the biggest announcements some of you may have heard; the Dominican Fathers made plans to build a religious retreat on Charles Island. We need all the help we can get, so if you would like to volunteer, please stay after services today to write your name on the sign-up sheet in the back of the church. The next announcement is that services will be held outside next weekend as long as no inclement weather arrives. May the Lord be with you."

"And with you too, Father," everyone chimed back. Everyone except for two people in the room…and I was one of them.

Green Eyes

6

"Aren't you coming?" Mother asked.

"I think I'll stay here a little longer and pray. I'll meet you back at home, okay?" I partially fibbed. I could tell she didn't believe it for a second, but nodded her head and smiled.

"Just come home before sunset," she warned. I nodded my head and kneeled back down, folding my hands together to continue praying. I wanted to be here alone to talk to Father although I felt like he was still out there somewhere with the rest of the people who were just leaving mass. Another part of me wanted to see who the man was and find out more about him. I peeked my eyes open to see if he was still sitting in the pew where he had been.

It was empty.

Was he even there to begin with, or had I just been seeing things like the pages turning on their own in my book?

I put my head down and continued my prayer in a whisper.

"Lord, rid me of the insanity my life has become. I'm trying my best, but things keep happening that I can't explain. There was a man that I saw, and I felt like I should know him...then he just vanished like everything and everyone else in my life. Lord, help me see the—"

"Now, if He helps you see the light, what happens if that light just so happens to be a fast-running train at the end of the tunnel coming right for you?" a man's voice interrupted my prayer. I jerked around to face the voice and saw the green eyes for a split second before he gently turned my head back to face forward again.

"What are you doing?" I whispered, wishing I could face him when I spoke.

"Answer my question," he insisted.

"Then at least my death will be quick," I answered, solemnly.

"That's no happy ending," he seemed surprised by my response.

"That's life for you..."

"Why were you watching me?" he asked.

"Same goes for you!" I covered my mouth, realizing I had broken out of a whisper.

"There's something about you…" he said.

"And why can't we face each other?" I continued staring before me, imagining his green eyes.

"Everyone will tell you I am bad news and think I am just trying to have my way with you."

"And what if everyone is right?" I asked.

"There's only one way to find out, isn't there?" he replied.

"Where do I know you from?" I asked, wishing he would let on more than he was telling me. He didn't respond, and I stood up and turned around, not caring who saw me speak with him. But the pew was empty. I looked at the exit of the church and saw him leaving.

When I walked out the same way, I looked left and right to find he was nowhere to be seen. I put my hand in my pocket to feel my compass like I always did when I felt lost in direction or in life in general.

I retraced my steps and went back into the church. I must have looked just as lost as I felt because the pastor came up to me and handed me a paper.

"There're still some open slots to sign up to volunteer, young lady," he said.

"Oh yes, I was looking for that… Thank you!" I placed it against the wall and wrote my name down reluctantly.

"The first meeting will be tomorrow morning. We look forward to seeing you there!" he exclaimed. I gave him a half-smile and headed out, not knowing what I had even gotten myself into.

Heading home, I wasn't sure what to think. The sun was barely setting, and I could've stayed out for far longer, but I knew the next day would be far longer than this one. I wasn't sure if I'd ever see those green eyes again and I don't know why I even wanted to, but there was one thing I knew for sure… I couldn't tell Mother I would be going out to the island. If she found out, she would forbid me because of the horrible stories the townspeople had passed down.

The warm summer air made it practically unbearable to walk back home as the sun beat down. On Sundays, everything was closed, so I walked by empty shops with their doors shut. I wished I had more courage to venture out here, but I felt like a hermit, as I was always home and rarely wanted to be in the public.

Tomorrow, I'd be venturing out to a place I had only heard stories about and never dreamed of actually going. A place that's history haunted me to my very core, but what haunted me more, most days, was the reality of life and the possibility I would never see Father again. I shook the thought from my mind that I normally kept in the back of my mind, shut behind all the walls that I could possibly put up. I needed a new focus, and that was this project I now signed up for. No matter how scary it seemed, it was nowhere close to what my life had become.

Curiosity

7

I felt an instant relief wash over me as I walked into the house. Finally, being in the shade from the blazing sun outside made me want to lie down and do absolutely nothing the rest of the day. I slowly sauntered up the stairs and switched out of my dress clothes to something that would feel much cooler on me. The other dress had practically clung to me like a glove, and I couldn't stay in it a second longer. When I walked over to the sink, I wet my hair and continued downstairs despite how dripping wet it now was. There was no place I'd be going and no one to see me, so it didn't really matter how I looked.

I took the compass out of the pocket from the old dress I had been wearing and sat it down on the dresser. It was amazing how objects had much more permanence than people did in this world. I turned my back on it, wishing it could guide me more than it had since I still felt lost no matter what in life. Wishing I could just go lie down in the bed beside the dresser, I knew I had to check on Mother and see how she was doing. It was much too early to go to sleep yet, anyway. When I went back downstairs, Mother had been sitting at the table.

"So, what did you stay after church for?" she asked, and I contemplated whether or not I should tell her. She knew about the island's past, so it was very possible she would forbid me from going. It was something for the church, though. Deep down, I hoped that man with green eyes may be there again. But even more importantly, I needed to figure out who the man was on the island that seemed to look out at me the other day. I felt like he was trying to tell me something, and the warning I gave to James was something I hadn't felt so strongly about since I could remember.

"I signed up to be a volunteer for the religious retreat that they're building," I admitted.

"Oh, that's wonderful! Isn't that on the Island, though?" Like clockwork, she said exactly what I thought she would.

"Yeah, but it's not like I'll be the only one there."

"Do you know anyone that will be there too?"

"Err…James, maybe?" I blurted out, knowing he hadn't signed up.

"Oh! Then that's perfect! You've known James for a while and he could protect you."

"Protect me from what?"

"Anyone…the island…?" she grimly said the last word as she looked down at the book in front of her. I walked over and sat down in the seat beside her to get a closer look at the book she had.

"People have always said the island was haunted… Your father would go out there very often and come back with all different types of findings. Sometimes arrowheads, other times keys that we didn't know what they would unlock and on rare occasions he would find remnants of the inn that used to be there."

She looked down at the book that was before her and gently slid it over to me and continued.

"This was your father's journal."

I felt my sunken heart lift as I scrambled to flip it open and read as fast as I could through the first few pages. There were drawings within the entries of what appeared to be some of his findings on the island. I closed it, feeling both overwhelmed and shaky, and hugged the journal close to my chest.

"Oh, thank you, Mother. Thank you so much! Why hadn't you given me this before??" I asked.

"He wanted me to wait until you were old enough and when you eventually sought out the island yourself. I had a feeling you would sign up to go there. Something about you and your father…the island has always drawn both of you there, no matter the risks."

"Why are you letting me go then?"

She stood up and took my hand in hers; her fingers sent an icy chill down my spine in the summer heat. I still sat there, feeling like I was five years old again and in trouble.

"There are some things in life you just need to find out for yourself and this is one of them."

Darkness

8

Darkness came fast and before I knew it, I found myself lighting candles so I could keep reading Father's journal entries. He spoke of the inn and how it was a vibrant place at one time. Only the most prestigious were able to stay there, but they would never find themselves going back there again. He never mentioned what happened there exactly, but did say the inn met its fiery demise. It was a question of how the fire started and most people thought it wasn't accidental at all, but no one heard from the woman who ran the inn, Lady Angeline, ever again after that. There was no news of a rebuild or reopening of the resort, either.

At the end of the entry about the inn, there was a small sketch he made of someone who appeared to be Lady Angeline. There was a veil over her head in it, but her eyes looked dark and sullen. At first glance, you'd think she was dressed for her wedding day, but how could any wedding day be this dreadful looking?

I kept flipping through pages and one stood out to me the most. It was his last entry before he left for the war. I will always remember that day as if it were etched into my soul.

June 5, 1917

My dearest Lucy,

I am leaving this journal with your mother. It is four o'clock in the early hours of the day and I have not told you or Mary that I've been called into service. I figured I would save you all the pain for as long as I possibly could. It is hard because you almost get scared when life is going well. You know that it is the calm before the storm. By now, you are older and can understand these things more. I want you to know it is okay to be scared. It is okay to anticipate the storm that is to come because if you are anything like your father, and I know straight to your stubborn core that you are...you will ride out any storm that comes your way. I leave later today; there is no refusing my country and I will protect it as I would my own flesh and blood. You will be safe on the farm. If you find yourself venturing out, make sure you never leave my compass behind. It will be the only thing that can guide you back home safely.

Lucy, no matter what it takes...I will come back for you and your mother. I promise.

Love, Father

The tears streamed down my cheeks onto the pages of his journal, partially smudging the ink. The letters in each word he wrote blurred from the splash of moisture. I quickly wiped my tears and left the book open to dry so as not to smudge even more of the ink. He knew all along he would be leaving, and we hadn't known until it was time for him to actually leave. For him to have kept that painful truth from us just to see us happy for the last moments that he could...that was true sacrifice. I wished I could go back to that date. I kept looking it over again and again. June 5th. June 5th. That was almost a decade ago and here I was in this same house with Mother, missing the third piece of the puzzle. Here I was, never giving any guy a chance because I was afraid they would leave and never come back, either.

But then it occurred to me.

If I had never had the relationship that I did with Father or even Mother, I would've never had any love in my heart at all. Mother and Father could have feared the inevitable what ifs, but if they gave into that fear then I would never be here. The risks we took were sometimes not worth it in the slightest, but it just takes the very few times that those risks come through as meaningful surprises that keep us going.

Tomorrow, I'd go to the island with the others and take that risk despite its wretched past. I would go there with a clean slate, and it would be a fresh day. If I didn't end up going, I would only ever live with that regret. I grabbed the pillow on my bed and hugged it close, wishing I didn't feel so alone for once.

Steps

9

The sun peeked in, illuminating the room that had once been dark and quiet. Now, birds chirped beside my bedroom window. Repetitive cheeps from the babies in their nests droned on as they yearned for food. I hid beneath the covers, trying to go back to sleep when I remembered what I signed up for. I wasn't even sure what time it was and jumped out of bed, despite how comfortable I had just been. Part of me wished I hadn't signed up for anything, but my curiosity about the monastery on the island and the mysterious man that awaited on the other side of the path sent my imagination wild. I rummaged through my closet, looking for something that would be light enough in this heat. Hopefully today it would be more cloudy. They told us to be there for 7 a.m. promptly because the tides would likely be lower at that time. I glanced out the window and felt an instant relief to see some clouds concealing the sun for a brief time. More seemed to be on the way.

Most of my dresses were more suitable for church and not going out to work—whatever that entailed, I did not know. I took out a yellow sundress that went to my knees and quickly pulled it over my head. It had various floral designs on it; carnations, lilies, and other flowers embroidered over the bright yellow. Along the lower neckline was a white piece of fabric that tied in the very front. The short sleeves made me feel cool, and I hoped it was a good choice. Looking into the mirror, my hair was quite a mess. It still had the curls from church the previous day, but they were tangled. I ran my fingers through them and tried to untangle the chaos myself, but gave up after just a few seconds and settled on brushing it back so I could pull it back in a bun.

When I got downstairs, Mother had a pastry waiting for me with a cup of tea. I could see her silhouette just through the curtain to the back porch. She was sitting outside looking out as she commonly would. It was almost as if she would wait there hoping that Father would just come walking down the road someday. I thought of those baby birds in the tree and how much they relied on their mother. In all this confusion that life had become, I could at least be thankful for the fact that I still had her. I drank half of the tea and grabbed Father's old canteen that I had cleaned and filled with water to bring along with me.

Just before I headed out the door, I noticed the book open on the table to another passage this time. I wasn't sure if Mother had left this open purposely for me to read or if she left it from her morning read. Either way, I took a moment to skim through the words.

(Proverbs 16:9)

In their hearts humans plan their course, but the Lord establishes their steps.

I pondered this for a moment. I wasn't sure what my course was in life yet, but wished that I knew. Losing

Father made it difficult to plan much of a future because of the unknown. Each step I took could have been either the good or bad things that happened while trying to get to where we wanted to be in life.

"Aren't you going to have your pastry?" The back door creaked open and Mother peeked her head in to ask. Before I could answer, she was already walking toward the pastry with a kitchen towel to wrap it in. She opened the bag I had on my shoulder, placing it inside.

"Thank you, Mom," I said.

"Don't come back too late, okay?" she said. "I talked with James, and he seemed quite confused about having signed up to volunteer. I made sure he understood." She winked. I felt the redness fill my cheeks as it had with a painful sunburn; she must have realized I had just made it up that he was going. When I opened the door, there he was, waiting.

"I won't. I love you," I said and hugged Mother, not even having any excuse to explain my fib this time.

"Love you too," she said, walking out onto the front porch with me, waving as James and I left.

"So...I apparently signed up for this?" he asked.

"You did? There's some irony there because I signed up too," I said.

"Lucy...I didn't! But Mary thinks I did." He stopped in his tracks as we walked down the road. I continued walking, but realized he was no longer beside me, so I stopped a few steps ahead of him and turned back.

"Okay, okay. I figured she trusts you and would feel more comfortable if she knew I was at least going with someone I knew. Anyway, you said your crew would be doing more work there soon. Today, you were going to go boating with them, no?"

"But why are you going in the first place? Do you even know what it entails?" He picked up his pace and caught up with me as I began walking again.

"No, but that's the fun in it. Hey, did you see that guy staring back at me in church the other day?" I decided to mention Green Eyes. James always went to church with his mother, too. It was a small town. Everyone knew everyone, but for some reason, that man was new. New to me anyway.

"You mean the guy you were staring at, drooling?"

"Hey!" I slapped him on the arm.

"Yes, I saw him," he said, laughing.

"Who is he?" I urged on, knowing full well James already knew I was interested. But was it that obvious? I had thought he was looking back at me the whole time. Then, he just disappeared…

"He is actually part of a tribe. They used to own the land there, so there have been some disputes about what should be done with the land. They come to the church sometimes as their people assimilated with the English when they first settled here."

My curiosity only raised even more questions; I wanted to know more.

"I would just leave it be. The tribespeople had warned us about the island, but it's so nice out there. I'm not sure why they would be saying anything…they just want their land back."

"But they're right. It was theirs, wasn't it?"

"Yeah, but what can we do now?"

"That's awful. Imagine if someone took everything you worked long and hard for."

"You're right, Lucy. We're making a nice place out of it, though. And they can still come too. I think you should just stay away from him."

"Seems so scary when we're the ones who took away things from them and we're the monsters…."

"Yep, you're going to ignore me anyway, aren't you?" James clearly read my mind.

"It doesn't hurt getting to know him." I smiled. As we drew closer to the beach, a crowd of people appeared on the very edge of the coastline and at the beginning of the pathway that led right to the island. The path wasn't there when I had gone there before, but now it was fully exposed. I wandered up to them and in the very center was the priest.

"We are glad to have you here with us and thank you so much for volunteering. Some of this will be hands-on work, like gardening, pulling weeds, and surveying the area. We have the areas marked off for the different buildings already."

He walked over to the beginning of the pathway as we all followed. When he turned back, he continued.

"We will try to stay together, but we need to make sure we have a headcount by 8:15. We'll head back at that time because when the tide comes in, the pathway will no longer be here. The only way we would be able to get back to the mainland is by boat.

"Okay, let's organize groups. Sam, you can be in charge of planting this bag of fresh bulbs around the shrine." He handed a bag that appeared to be quite heavy to who I assumed to be Sam. He was one of the speakers that frequently said the readings before the priest said the gospel and homily in church.

"Next up, we need some people to dig the holes and pull weeds for the bulbs. Sam will just be putting them out, but you will need to dig the holes for them." Several lanky men offered themselves up for that job. Including Green Eyes.

Ghost

10

For some reason, it was as though there was something pulling me to him. I felt myself stepping forward, too, toward the others who had volunteered to shovel and realized they were all men except for a select few of us. They all started laughing, except for Green Eyes. He just smiled and shook his head.

"Okay, little lady. I appreciate the courage, but you haven't even come dressed for all the heavy lifting and dirty work this group is about to do. You can plant the flowers," one of them said.

"I work on a farm. Digging a few holes is something I think I can handle." I stood my ground.

"If you say so!" They handed me a shovel right away, and I took it with pride. I saw James head over to Sam and could've sworn he was going to join my group, but when I saw his childhood crush, Ann, it was clear why he chose that group.

We walked down the rocky pathway and I could feel the rocks pushing further and further into the soles of my thin shoes with each step. I winced through the pain and kept my eyes on the island before all of us. Everyone went ahead of me and I felt like it would take forever to catch up. Luckily, there was a cool breeze from being on the water and the blazing sun was still hidden behind the clouds.

"Do you want some help?" the familiar voice asked from behind me. I hadn't realized there was anyone even back there. They must have seen how slow I was going.

"Of course not." I bit my lip, wishing I wasn't so stubborn and could accept the help for once.

"You look like you're struggling there quite a bit," Green Eyes persisted.

"And how would you suggest I am helped?" I refused to look back and kept moving forward. I wanted to know more about him, but James was right. I had to be cautious.

In the next second, I felt arms swoop me up from behind. I clung to my shovel and tried not to knock him out with it.

"What are you doing?!"

"Helping you; stop squirming." He moved me much faster than I had been walking. I really was struggling back there. The moment of relief for my feet felt like pure heaven. I had work shoes back at home, but being out in public as a lady was stressful because I felt we were always expected to have formal clothes of some sort on.

"What if the others see?" I asked, hoping my dress was long enough to conceal me.

"Who cares about the others? If they ask, you hurt your feet and I was helping you," he said. I turned my head away from the island and looked straight into his eyes. He was clean shaven and had such dark, dark hair despite the light in his eyes.

"Do you see something you like?" he asked and I couldn't help but roll my eyes, turning back away.

"Well, apparently *you* do. You scooped me up and refuse to put me down."

"Okay, okay…fine, fine. I will put you down." He walked over to the edge of the path and held me over the water.

"DON'T YOU DARE!!" I shouted, prompting the others to look behind them. They shook their heads and laughed. Green Eyes continued on, showing it was just a bluff. We finally walked up to the island, and he placed me down. I walked away in a huff with my shovel, aggravated by the nerve he had. But I couldn't be too upset because he was 'helping' me, after all.

When I looked over my shoulder, he was just standing there with his arms crossed, staring out at me. I turned and gestured at him as if shooing him away.

Following the outside of the island, it felt much larger than it had appeared when I had been on the mainland. I didn't want to be seen with Green Eyes any more than I had already been—it was a small town and people would surely start talking if they weren't already. The other mysterious man that I saw crept back into my mind. He seemed much older than I. Thoughts about Green Eyes went to the back of my mind as I now pondered who the other man could have been and if he was okay or had been stranded. As I continued walking, I noticed they had already built several buildings on the island, and I could easily pick out which house would be the place of worship. There was a stone archway with a statue of Mary Magdalene in the center. I looked up at her, knowing how hopeful she had been even in the worst of times. I felt like someone was following me, so I picked up my pace and went more quickly, in and out of the various trees that stood tall. I started making my way toward the center of the island so I could lose him more quickly. After moving farther and farther in and using the shovel as a walking stick, the sound of the crowd chattering faded and the only sound that remained was of the twigs snapping and leaves crunching under my feet. I happened upon what appeared to be a shrine. I ran my fingers over each stone and felt a shock go through me as I did. It was as if I had jumped in ice cold water except, I was completely dry. I felt like I had been here before. I looked back out at where I had come from and there was nothing but trees. Nothing but trees and... a tall man walking the opposite way. He looked to be the same man I saw from far away that day. This time, he wasn't holding a bag. When I saw him, I could tell he was wearing a uniform of some sort, but wasn't close enough to make it out. From this distance, it appeared to be a military uniform. But he was walking the other way still.

"Wait!" I called out after him.

I tried to catch up with him, but the faster I went, the more quickly he walked away. I followed him all the way back to the edge of the island where the waters met its sandy beaches. He was standing with his feet in the water when he finally turned back, clearly aware I was chasing him this entire time. I felt like my heart stopped at the sight of him. My mind couldn't comprehend how he was here after all this time. I blinked my eyes, and he was still there, saying nothing at all. Father's warm and welcoming eyes stared back at me for one second and in the next, the entirety of his being seemed to vanish into thin air. I rushed to the spot he had just stood, and an X was drawn into the sand. I dropped the shovel and paced back and forth over the X, looking all around for him desperately, falling to my knees. He had just been there. He was finally back. The day I had been waiting for almost my entire life had come and vanished in an instant before I could even fully process it. I held my face in my hands as I sobbed uncontrollably and wished I had never even come here. The strange occurrences in the church and seeing the man from far away who turned out to be Father; I had gone insane. But I know what I saw. I could hear twigs crunching from behind me and feet pressing into the sand with each step. I didn't care to look this time because I knew it wouldn't be him. It was too good to be true. I put my head back in my hands, wishing I could hide myself from the world. Wishing I could conceal myself from the constant pain that tore at my heart.

"I'm here," Green Eyes said, getting down on his knees and hugging me close to him.

"He was just here. I was so close." Saying it out loud made me sob even more.

"Who was?" he asked.

"It doesn't even matter. I thought I saw someone I knew, but I guess that was just my mind playing tricks on me…"

"And you saw him right here?" He pulled away and looked me directly in my eyes.

"I'm not joking. I don't even know who you are, so I don't know why I'm telling you all this," I said.

"Jack. My name is Jack, and it's nice to meet you…Lucy," he said.

"But how do you know who I am?" I asked.

"I saw your name on the list of volunteers after you signed it. Now tell me who you saw…"

"You can't tell anyone, but I somehow saw my father, who had been missing for years after he was drafted into the war."

Secret

11

"Now faith is the assurance of things hoped for, the conviction of things not seen."

(Hebrews 11:1)

"Your secret is safe with me." He put out his hand to help me back up.

"What?" I was stunned at his response and took his hand less reluctantly than I thought I would. "You believe me?"

"Come here while we escape the work that we signed up for." He led me to a large rock that was big enough for both of us to sit on. I sat, feeling more at ease with his presence by my side.

"I know you don't know me, but there are some things you need to know about this island," he said.

Great, he didn't even believe me. It was likely he was going to tell everyone I was seeing things and then I would surely be locked up. When I tried to move to the right or the left to go around him, he mirrored my movements.

"Lucy, stop!" he said firmly. "You didn't give me a chance to finish. You're right. I hadn't believed anything I heard either. It sounds ridiculous, but Lucy..." He took both of my hands in his. "Lucy, when I would come out here, strange things happened."

I let my hands go limp in his and stopped trying to leave. His voice was sincere and the honesty in his eyes was something no one could just make up.

"I lost both my mother and father at a young age…and when I was sitting on that rock back there like I just had with you, I saw them just appear. I tried to follow them, but then they just vanished. Just like that, they were gone."

"Are you telling me the truth?" I asked.

"Why would I make this up?" His green eyes seemed to stare into my soul. In that instant, I felt like I knew this stranger after all.

"What happened after they disappeared?"

"What do you mean?"

"Did you see anything that seemed to have been left by them?"

"You know what... yeah. I saw Xs traced in the sand."

I immediately ran back to the X from before and it was gone. It, too, had disappeared as if it were never there to begin with.

"Lucy."

"Jack?"

"Something drew me to you in that church, and I want to learn more about you. I want to know about the man you saw. But I didn't want anyone to see us together because I was afraid someone would tell you to steer clear of me."

My mind went to James immediately. His warnings may still prove to be true, but I couldn't help but give Jack an ounce of trust for confiding in me. It was sad people seemed to shut others out just because they were different. In our world, everyone seemed to push one another to be the same. More of the same sounded awful boring to me.

"I can't talk about him…yet. It is very hard to speak about my father because it just makes his disappearance that much more real to me." I looked down at the sand, feeling a single tear stream down my cheek.

"When you're ready, you can talk. There's no one forcing you to do anything." He put his hand under my chin and tilted my face up so I was looking at him again.

"I really saw him."

"I know. Me too."

Hope

12

"**F**or in this hope we were saved. Now hope that is seen is not hope. For who hopes for what he sees? But if we hope for what we do not see, we wait for it with patience."

(Romans 8:24-25)

Hope. It is the single thing that keeps every person going no matter where they came from or what their backstory is. To have hope helps us to keep going no matter what trials and tribulations any one person has gone through. It is said that the people who were prisoners of war survived merely on this one word. If not, the mind would slowly fall into a vegetative state.

All along, I had hope that Father would come back and a big part of me still believed that to be true. It has been that hope that has kept me going. When I saw him, I could feel my heart leap up in my chest as I realized the day had finally come and everything would be set right again. But realizing it was either my own mind playing tricks on me or something else I can't explain made me question that hope I had felt for so very long. The distrust that had grown in me of not knowing when and if Father would be back had easily transferred to other relationships in my life. I couldn't help but feel skeptical of Jack's true intentions. Part of me wanted to believe he, too, saw Father and everything he was telling me was true, but I kept hearing that word over and over in my head: Cautious.

"Jack!!! Lucy!!!" We heard them calling and hadn't realized how much time had passed.

I looked at Jack and his bulged eyes likely matched my own.

"The pathway!" I shouted, remembering how the tide would come in and conceal it completely, leaving us trapped there until the next hour of low tide.

"Let's go!" He grabbed my hand, and we ran down the sandy coast of the island, heading back around to the crowd. They had packed up all of their things in bags and were already heading down the pathway.

"Where were you guys?!" James yelled back as he was one of the last ones that hadn't yet stepped foot on the pathway that led back to the mainland.

Before I could speak, Jack had already managed to come up with a better excuse than I could ever have.

"She got lost in the forest looking for one of the shrines and I found her. I had to help her back over. She didn't exactly wear the right shoes..." he said.

"Uh huh," James replied.

I could tell James didn't believe it for a second as he shook his head and turned back to Ann, starting down the path. Water had already started filling over the rocks and sand; high tide was coming.

"Do you want me to help you get across again?" Jack asked.

"I think I am good, thanks." I struggled to move past him, but made it a point that I didn't need any more of his help. I was afraid of getting too close to him and was hesitant as to whether or not he was even telling the truth. I could feel the water as it pooled into my shoes. With each step, my feet felt heavier, almost as if I were lifting cement.

"Okay…whatever you say." He let out a chuckle and continued on, nearing closer to James up ahead.

I couldn't tell what they were saying, but I knew Jack started talking with James as they both looked back at me and started laughing.

"Lucy, quit being stubborn. Just let him help you!" The change in James's tone toward Jack was like night and day. Whatever Jack said to him must have worked, because it definitely earned his liking for the time being.

"I'll ask for help when I need it. Thank you very much." I attempted going faster to show I was more than capable. In the next second, I went sliding down and nearly landed in a complete split. The shooting pain came sudden and fast as I realized I cut up my legs on the sharp rocks with my fall. I wanted to scream in pain, but bit my tongue as I struggled to get back up. When I looked up, they were all continuing on and much farther ahead. The salt from the water made the pain even worse as it filled my cuts. I picked up the end of my dress to look at the damage and found a large gash on the side of my leg. What was more alarming than the pain that I felt was the shape of my wound. It was an X just as the island's mark that seemed to have disappeared.

I looked back up and caught both Jack's and James's eyes. They ran back toward me and by this time, the path was barely visible. Waves washed over and concealed it bit by bit.

"Why didn't you just let him help you?" James asked, pulling my right arm around him to help me up, but between the sight of blood and pain, I was so lightheaded that I could barely walk.

"Do you mind if I...?" Jack asked as he took the bloodied edge of my dress in his hands.

"Just go ahead." I didn't know what he was going to do, but didn't care at this point. He tied the side of my dress in a knot and got his canteen out, emptying it over my wound. The sudden relief in pain as the salt left my skin caused me to feel dizzy. The world felt as if it were spinning around me. I could've sworn I saw stars. Jack was mouthing something, but all I could see were those green eyes. In the next moment, everything went black.

The Inevitable

13

“**B**e sober-minded; be watchful. Your adversary the devil prowls around like a roaring lion, seeking someone to devour.”

(Peter 5:8)

Darkness. It was inevitable for us all, but we never knew when eternal darkness would quite come. And in life, one would find themselves feeling like they were in a state of complete darkness, no matter how much light seemed to be in their life. I opened my eyes to find myself in my bed somehow. I flinched immediately when I saw a figure sitting to my right, finally calming down as I realized it was just Mother in her rocking chair. She seemed to be watching me like a hawk and shot right up as soon as I tried to lift myself up into a sitting position.

"Where is he?" was the first thing I asked.

"Who?"

The shooting pain came in my legs, reminding me of my fall, and I lay back down on the bed.

"How did I get back here?" I asked.

"James brought you back, of course. Who else would?" She looked just as confused as me.

"Oh, I don't know..." I didn't feel like explaining.

Deciding that I looked like I was going to be okay, Mother's scolding began…

"What were you doing dressing the way you did and going out on the rocky sandbar? What did you think?" she asked. "Your father knew that island was no good. I think it's best you stay away."

"I can't! They need my help!" I protested.

"Well, you weren't much help today, were you?" She made a point, but after the things I saw there…I had to go back.

"It's just with the church group. I'll be fine. I'll wear better shoes next time."

"Lucy, there won't be a next time. I need help here on the farm, anyway."

With that, she left the room and closed the door behind her, ending any possibility of negotiating with her any further. And there I was, alone with my endless thoughts, without the ability to do anything at all. Thinking of Jack and what he was doing right now…and how stubborn I was to not just let him carry me on the way back. I wouldn't have been in this position and now would never see him again. There was something about him that was unlike the others. He seemed to have come from nowhere, but it was as if he had always been here. We both had the connection of losing our loved ones, and something drew us to each other like magnets.

I stared at the bedroom door, wishing he would come in instead of Mother. He'd somehow sneak past her and sit at the edge of the bed, causing my heart to jump out of my chest. I could only imagine how much it would race. When he moved closer to me, he'd run his fingers through my hair and kiss me on my forehead. Despite his calming green eyes, there was an intense darkness to him I couldn't quite place.

The candle that Mother left in the bedroom by my bedside abruptly went out, leaving me in absolute darkness other than the moonlight that cast its light through the window. Something scraped against the window, slowly opening it bit by bit. The cool summer night breeze drifted around me, sending a chill down my spine. The curtains concealed whatever lurked behind it just enough so I couldn't see exactly what it was, but there was a new shadow that contrasted greatly against the moonlight. This shadow seemed to have fingers and grabbed onto the edge of the curtain, blood dripping down, staining through. I felt like my heart was going to jump out of my chest and tried my best to stay quiet so I wasn't found, but felt as though whomever was breaking in could likely hear my heart thump too.

Its skeleton-like hand reached in farther and monstrous fangs peered in, revealing part of its wolf-like face. It stared down at me, drooling as if I were its next snack. At that point, I couldn't hold it in any longer.

"HELP!!!!!" I screamed, unable to leave my bed, sheets seeming to swallow me whole. I felt like I was being choked as I squeezed my eyes shut, not wanting to take another look at the monster.

"I'm here, I'm here," I heard Mother's voice. She was shaking me again and again. I reluctantly opened my eyes and looked right at the window to find the beast was gone. When I looked back at Mother, I wanted to warn her. I felt like we needed to get out of here as soon as possible. But would she believe me?

"We need to leave. We're not safe. Please."

"What happened? We're fine. You just had a bad dream, that's all," she assured me and helped me sit up so she could rub my back in circles like she did when I was just a child and would awaken from nightmares.

"You shouldn't have opened up the window. Maybe that's why you had a nightmare, Lu…" As soon as she walked over, I nearly jumped out of bed without thinking of the gashes in my legs that still pained me.

"No!!" I screamed so she wouldn't go any closer, but it was too late—she had already closed the window and walked back over my way, looking at me as if I should be taken to the madhouse.

The thing was, I already felt like I was in one…

Nightmare

14

"And without faith it is impossible to please him, for whoever would draw near to God must believe that he exists and that he rewards those who seek him."

(Hebrews 11:6)

I stayed up as long as I could, but at some point the night took me over and before I knew it, light was already creeping in through that same window that darkness just had. I pulled the covers over my head, wishing I could stay invisible forever.

"Lucy, you have a visitor!" Mother yelled from downstairs. But how in the world did she expect me to get dressed and come all the way down in such little time? I stumbled out of bed and limped on my good leg over to the mirror. I nearly jumped out of my skin at my reflection. I was as pale as a ghost and my hair was a complete mess.

"He's going to come up, alright? Just your friend checking in on you," she called up. How dare she let someone come up! This was so aggravating. I could hear every step 'he' took up the stairs. I stumbled over to my dresser and slipped out of my nightgown and quickly placed a long cotton dress over my head, heading back to the mirror to spray perfume a few times, as I hadn't bathed just yet.

They gently knocked on the door and, before I could respond, Jack pushed the door in and looked at me with worried eyes.

"Are you okay, Lucy?" He ran over to me in an instant and assessed my arms and legs as if he were a doctor checking his patient.

"Why wouldn't I be okay? It was just a silly, clumsy fall yesterday."

"I just thought something happened last night and you may have been hurt…"

My thoughts instantly went to the beast that I tried to lock in the back of my mind. I shivered despite how warm it already was and looked over to the window, then back at Jack. I wasn't sure how much I could tell him, so I decided to keep my lips sealed and stumbled over to the window, staring at it, and wondered how it could have just been a nightmare. Lost in thought, I hadn't realized the tears streaming down my cheeks until Jack came before me and wrapped his arms around me.

I pressed my lips into his chest and squeezed my eyes, and for a brief moment, I could escape the puzzle that life was. When I opened my eyes again, I saw a trace of something dark at the very edge of the curtain. Beyond that was a scratch against the windowsill, as if something tried to claw its way in.

"Take me away from here." I looked into Jack's mesmerizing eyes.

"What did you see?" He looked at the window, then back at me. I wanted to tell him everything, but felt that if I said it, it would have made the nightmare that much more real.

"I don't know how to say it," I admitted.

"I'm here. You don't have to worry now. You can tell me anything."

"What if you don't believe me?"

"I feared the same exact thing when I came here. Look, there's something I need to tell you…" he said. I walked over to the edge of the bed and sat down, staring up at him.

"Tell me."

"Ever since I came back here to this small town, I had been having nightmares almost every single night. And last night…you were in one of them. There was nothing I could do; it was as if I were just a fly on the wall, but there was a beast that tried coming in your window. My hands were tied, and that powerless feeling was a nightmare enough because I wanted to save you more than anything. When I woke up, it felt like it had been so real that I had to check on you."

"Jack," was all I could say.

"You don't believe me." He looked down at the ground and began walking out of my bedroom.

I hopped over to him on my good leg and pulled him toward me.

"I had the same nightmare; except I lived it…"

Vulnerable

15

Just then, another knock came on the door. Again, before I could respond, James came through and looked at Jack, then I, back and forth as if he couldn't believe we were together, and Jack had reached me first.

"Does anyone knock anymore or give fair warning?!" I shouted, putting my hands on my hips in disbelief. Even though I thought of James as a brother, it still would have been nice.

"I am assuming you're okay then." James looked down at the ground.

"Yeah, thank you James. I appreciate both of you. Honestly, I think I just need some time to myself right now." I wobbled over to the door and they both went to catch me. And in that moment, I could see the jealousy in Jack's eyes that I had never seen before. Jealousy peeled over those once sensitive and soft green eyes and masked them in a hatred that I hadn't even known he was capable of.

He turned back to me, and his eyes softened.

"I will see you later."

Without so much as acknowledging James in any way, Jack walked out of the room and brought the tension with him out as soon as he left.

"Ehem," I cleared my throat, trying to get James to leave too. I was done with the day already, and it had only just begun. I looked over at the bed and wanted it to suck me back in somehow, but quickly glanced at the window and realized I had to get out.

"What's wrong?" James asked, completely oblivious to my signaling.

"I want to leave here and just get some space. I feel like I've been trapped in this room," I said, trying to limp my way over to the door.

"Doesn't look like you're getting anywhere, anytime soon," he laughed.

"Oh, just stay there. By all means…"

"Hey, what was that all about?"

"What?" I asked, knowing exactly what he was talking about, but still wanting to hear him say it.

"Jack came all the way here to check on you and then he left as soon as I came. What happened before I came in?" he asked.

"Oh, we were just talking about what happened. That's all…" I said, feeling my cheeks grow red at the thought of having been so close to him.

"Lu, you can't fool me."

"Don't you have to go bother Ann or something?" I asked, hoping to change the subject off of Jack.

"She's very good. Thank you for asking. I was planning to bring her for a picnic tomorrow."

"Did they call off the trip to the island by boat?" I asked, curious. Whenever the tide wasn't low enough to reveal the path, boats were available to bring people to and from the island.

"No, they just moved it tomorrow. But I'm going to be with Ann, so no worries, Lu. I know you have some kind of premonition that something is bound to go wrong."

"I don't know why, but I just feel like it isn't going to go as planned," I said, walking back to the edge of my bed, taking a seat and giving up on actually going anywhere.

James walked over to me and crossed his arms over his chest. This is what he did when he was about to say something serious.

"Lucy."

I nodded.

"You have been like a big sister to me ever since my father left. I just want you to be careful with this guy. We don't know him."

"I can take care of myself, James…"

"There's just something off about this guy. I can't place it, but just be on your guard," James said as he walked out the door, leaving me to my thoughts, which could prove to be one of the most dangerous things.

I walked over to the window and saw the scrapes from before on the windowsill. I pressed my finger into one single claw mark and traced it up behind the curtain. When I pulled the curtain to the side, part of the engraving in the wall had a clear line of what appeared to be blood. I jumped back, scared of the reality that now was. There was no escaping whatever beast this was; even in my dreams it seemed to come. I wished I could talk to Father about this and that he could protect me. I felt so vulnerable, unprotected, and scared for my life.

I slowly walked over to my bedroom door, limping down the stairs slowly whilst holding on to the railing on the wall. When I got down, Mother wasn't downstairs anywhere. I crept toward the window and looked out back to find she was on her hands and knees beside the temporary grave we had made for Father. After James' father came back and we realized the war had already ended and still, he hadn't come home…we needed closure and wanted to let his soul rest at peace no matter where he was. I knew both of us were still very much in denial that he was actually not coming back. We both had a sliver of hope that we hung on to each day, and I was sure every time she looked out the front of our home, she too looked for Father right away. At first, neither of us wanted to leave the house for fear he would come home to an empty house. We would switch on and off to go to church each week, but after we had the closure of the funeral for him and said our "goodbyes," we started to attend church together again.

I walked outside to join her, and she hadn't seemed to notice I was there yet. I limped all the way beside her and kneeled. She looked over at me with tears in her eyes and picked up her arm, revealing a long gash that had definitely not been there the day before. The only thing I could think of was how perfectly it matched the claw mark on the window in my bedroom.

The Beast

16

"And I saw a beast rising out of the sea, with ten horns and seven heads, with ten diadems on its horns and blasphemous names on its heads. And the beast that I saw was like a leopard; its feet were like a bear's, and its mouth was like a lion's mouth. And to it the dragon gave his power and his throne and great authority. One of its heads seemed to have a mortal wound, but its mortal wound was healed, and the whole earth marveled as they followed the beast."

(Revelation 13:1-8)

Even the most vicious of creatures seem to lead its prey directly toward itself, barely having to search or hunt for its next victims. I felt that my duty to my father to look after Mother was null and void as soon as I saw the mark on her arm. All along, I had been worried that she wouldn't believe me and there she was going through the exact same thing as I had been.

"When were you going to tell me?" was all I could ask despite the many questions that stay lingering on my tongue.

"Lucy, there are many things you still do not yet know of…and it has been for your own safety."

"And how do you suggest this is keeping me safe when it has come right to my very room at night?" I stood up, placing my hands on my hips, frustrated and worried at the same time.

"What do you think drew Father to the island so often? He would try to track down the beast, but never did it get as close as your chambers."

"And what brought it so close, then?" I asked.

"All I could think of was that beast must have gotten a whiff of your scent and is now tracking you," she replied, standing up beside Father's grave and looking at me right in the eye.

"Where do you suppose it 'caught a whiff' of me?" I couldn't believe what I was even saying.

"The island."

"It comes from the island?" I asked. "I went directly to the middle and saw no such thing..." My mind went to the sight of Father.

"But did you see anything else?" she asked.

"Like what?" I was not giving in just yet.

"Like someone or something that couldn't possibly be there...but was?"

I didn't answer, and the silence was deafening. When I shrugged my shoulders, I knew she wouldn't take that for an answer. She could read right through me.

"Lucy, you need to tell me. No matter how crazy it may seem."

"I saw Father, alright? I saw Father." I crossed my arms over my chest and felt the tear creep down my cheek. Before I could wipe it away, she had already walked over toward me and pressed her fingers against the side of my face, wiping the tear away for me. Her deep blue eyes were full of worry and concern as she took my hands in hers.

"Oh, dear…" was all she could muster out.

"What?"

"You are its next victim."

"How are you so sure?? What do you mean?" I nearly became frantic and wanted to run for the hills, but wasn't sure that was even safe. Was I safe anywhere at all?

"This beast finds whatever is dearest to you…it lures you in with it and before you know it, you are trapped on the island for it to take."

"But I don't understand. Why wouldn't it have just taken me already?" I asked.

"It comes out at night and must feast on the island. It had come here that night to take you back with it…" She looked down, shaking her head. "Oh, I have failed your father…"

"Mother, how could you possibly have controlled this?" I asked.

"I should have told you sooner. I thought keeping this from you would have saved you the curiosity."

"So why did I see Father then?"

"You want to see your father again more than anything in this world. By showing you that Father is on the island, the beast knew you would come back again and again."

And what she said was true. I was desperate to see him again, and I had thought about going there again just to find him. I felt more exposed than ever.

"There is nowhere I am safe," I said, goosebumps forming along my arms and legs as I began to realize my certain fate.

Hope

17

"Fear not, for I am with you; be not dismayed, for I am your God; I will strengthen you, I will help you, I will uphold you with my righteous right hand."

(Isaiah 41:10)

The unknown can be crippling in the sense it will cause you to remain stagnant in the endless cycle that your life has been. One would much rather stay with what they have been most familiar with as opposed to try something that they never had before. But there are times curiosity can get the best of you and the path that you find yourself down leads you to not even recognize yourself any longer. That is the true horror; when you have lost yourself.

I stayed in Mother's chambers after that night and refused to go back to my own. Day after day, I had not heard from James or Jack. It was like they had disappeared off the face of the earth. Then one morning, a knock came at the door. It startled both Mother and me, but finally my leg was in better shape to walk again, so I walked over to answer the door.

James stood there, his hair disheveled and entire attire out of sorts. I could feel my eyebrows furrow in, confused. Without even having to ask, he walked right past me and started pacing back and forth.

"Lucy, you were right—you were right—you were right," was all he kept saying. Mother nor I had the slightest clue and if I could have guessed, the heat must have surely gotten to him.

"Go on…" I insisted, going back to sit down at the table while I waited for him to collect himself.

"You didn't hear?!" His voice raised abruptly as he walked right over to me.

"Hear what?"

"You know that boat you told me not to take to the island? The entire lot of the crew—gone! An unexplainable capsizing of a simple, short ride from the mainland to the island… they're still looking for bodies."

I looked at Mother right away, and she was as shocked as I.

"You were supposed to be on that boat," I said, not knowing what else to say or do.

"You saved my life, Lucy."

"But how?"

"You warned me. How did you know, though?" He asked a question even I could not have answered.

"I really don't know. I just had a feeling," was all I could say.

"Have you seen Jack?" I asked, immediately worried if he was supposed to be on that same boat.

"Come to think of it…no, no, I have not. The last I visited you, he was acting a bit off and then seemed to have stormed out. I thought he would have surely been back to check on you."

"Oh, God… he may have been on that boat, James."

I immediately felt sick to my stomach, like there was a knife digging into me and turning in circles. But there was nothing I could do. I couldn't pull the knife out or bandage the wound because it was only within me, in my heart.

"I need to find him," I said, not caring what the repercussions were.

"James, please go with her. She won't listen to me even if I tell her not to go. She will find a way. Just go with her!" Mother called out, but I was already headed out the door and I knew exactly where I had to go.

"I will," I heard him reply to her. I didn't bother to look back; I just wanted to get to the coastline more than anything.

The sun's bright rays were concealed by dark storm clouds. There was not a bird in sight in the sky and I felt like the sky would open up at any moment. The adrenaline rushing through me caused me to completely forget about the pain that had once shot through my leg from walking on it. At first, I walked as fast as I could. As I kept thinking about Jack and the possibility that he was hurt, I broke into a run.

"Lucy!!!" James called after me. I didn't care. I wasn't waiting for him. Part of me didn't even want him to follow me. I felt like I had to do this alone. I ran into the bushes that separated the beach from the dirt roads. When I broke through on the other side, I realized I had lost James completely and was grateful he was no longer in sight of me.

I treaded closer to the edge of the coast, finding that it must have been low tide as the rocky path was fully formed to go to the island. This time, I was thankful I wore my work boots. I couldn't run as fast since the rocks were a bit slippery, but I heard the shells crush underneath each step I took. Every time I crushed another shell, I felt like it was my heart sinking deeper in my chest. I needed to find him.

I hadn't quite prepared myself for the outcome yet. Despite all the hopeless turns my life had taken, the hope for Jack to be alive still lingered in my heart. I hadn't even thought of the beast since finding him was the most important thing right then.

18

"He causes his sun to rise on the evil and the good, and sends rain on the righteous and the unrighteous."

(Matthew 5:45)

As I drew closer to the island, the rain came down that much harder. I scaled to the right and left and looked every which way; desperate to find him anyway I could. In the short time I knew him, he gave me the hope that

I needed. The time on the island with him flashed back through my mind. He might have been the only other person who saw what I saw out there. We held that connection that I hadn't with anyone else. And for some odd reason, I felt I hadn't just recently met him. I felt he had been here all along my entire life.

But what happens with everyone that I hold close and dear to me? They leave or get hurt in some way. I couldn't take another person leaving. The heartbreak was eating me alive. It nearly made me not want to form any relationships with anyone or even talk to anyone at all.

After circling the island continuously, I dropped to my knees and let the rain pour on me. Tears streaming down my cheeks, just adding to the relentless rain that showered down. I looked out at the water and wished I could just walk in, and the seas would swallow me whole. The waves crashed, matching exactly how I felt in the moment. I should've just gone back down the path, but I didn't want to have to face the inevitable of having to accept yet another person gone. I wasn't exactly sure what I even expected by coming out here, but for some reason I felt the island had answers for me despite its horrors.

I pressed my hands into the sand and gathered a bunch, forming a ball I could squeeze, and it would just disintegrate. My dress clung to my skin and was completely soaked. It was almost as if I had just gotten out of the bath since my hair was drenched as well.

"He's gone...just like you too, Dad," I said it aloud and it made it that much more real.

"Who's gone?" A voice came from behind me. I quickly turned around to find green eyes staring back at me. We were about two arms' length distance from one another.

I couldn't help but run into his arms, at which point he picked me up. We were both soaking wet from the rain, but at that point, it didn't even matter anymore. I felt my heart lifted high in my chest.

He held me close in his arms and put one arm under my legs as he looked into my eyes. Worry filled his own.

"I thought you were gone," I said, not knowing if the tears streaming down my cheeks were from the rain or my eyes.

"Where would I go?" he asked.

"The boat capsized…and I hadn't seen you." I pressed my head into his chest, wishing I could just curl and warm up right next to him.

"I'm okay, we're both okay," he reassured me.

He took me in his arms and carried me inward on the island. We went past several buildings, and he brought me to the very center where the main church was. We went inside to find empty pews, but I was thankful for the shelter from the storm. He gently released me from his hold onto the back pew.

"I kept my distance from you because I didn't want you to get hurt more than you already had."

"And how would that happen?" I asked the obvious question as he sat beside me. We were completely alone in this church, probably because no one wanted to come out in the pouring rain and aside from that, they hadn't even officially opened their doors yet to the public.

"Lucy, I think I am bad luck to you. It seems wherever I go, that monster follows..."

"Monster?" I knew exactly what he was talking about, but didn't realize he knew so much.

"The beast that left that mark on your window."

"You'd be silly to think that you're the cause of all this!" I turned my whole body toward him. Something about those green eyes drew me in, but he kept looking down for some reason. I couldn't quite place it. It was almost as if he was ashamed of himself.

"I just feel like I had. Rumor says that the beast has been lurking Charles Island for as long as anyone can remember...even when the natives, my ancestors, had ownership of its grounds. But it wasn't used as a place to live, really…"

"Then what did they use it for?"

"It was called Poquahaug. This means 'Sacred Land.'"

"So why are we building on it if it's pretty much cursed?" I asked, confused as to how no one seemed to notice that.

"They don't believe in it and don't listen. They do not see the things that you and I have."

My cheeks felt flush as I felt myself turning bright red in the face. The fact that he named the connection we both share made me want to lean in and become even closer with him.

"Lucy," he finally looked up at me.

"Yes, Jack?" I looked back into his eyes.

"No matter how much I have tried to stay away from you... there is nothing that can keep us apart. And I don't want to be apart from you any longer."

"Then don't," I replied.

Believe

19

"Even to your old age and gray hairs I am he, I am he who will sustain you. I have made you and I will carry you; I will sustain you and I will rescue you."

(Isaiah 46:4)

It is interesting in life that we are always carried. Whether it be from when we were first born and carried in our mother's arms to our loved one's arms that we eventually build a life with, but in the very end we continue to be carried by God as we had been all along no matter what.

"Don't think for a second that I'm not carrying you the whole way back!" Jack laughed.

"I can walk myself, you know! I wore good shoes this time!!" I squirmed slightly in his arms.

"And we saw how well that worked out last time." He rolled his eyes.

"I mean, I've made it this far in life without you, love!" I playfully said back.

"Okay, if you insist..." He held me over the water and acted as if he were going to let go and just let me fall into the shallow, rocky depths.

"DON'T YOU DARE!" I screamed, giggling at the same time, knowing full well he wouldn't do that.

We continued down the path, and luckily, the rain had subsided. The sun was partially peeking out from behind the clouds. It was as though the weather matched my mood in the most perfect of ways.

"We're going to be late!" he said, picking up the pace with me still in his arms.

"Late for what, exactly?"

"Mass. It's Sunday!" he exclaimed.

"Uhm, there is no way I am going to mass dressed like this," I said, looking down at my muddy work boots and ripped up dress that still clung to my skin from the rain.

"We've got time for me to bring you home and then head over. We can go with your mother, too," he suggested.

The last thing I felt like doing was going to mass after that exhausting morning when I barely slept a wink as it was. HIs kind offers gave me no choice but to give in. When we finally got to my home, my dress had already dried. The rips and stains led me to throw it directly into the trash and deem it unwearable. I didn't even want to try to get the stains out of the dress.

"I'll be down here," Jack called up. When I walked up the stairs, I found Mother in my room, tracing her fingers against the claw mark on the window. I wondered how long she had been there.

"I found him."

"Oh!" She jumped, which was surprising because she could usually hear me coming.

"He wasn't on the boat when it capsized, thank God. He wants to come to church with us. I think we've all been through a lot, and we should go," I said.

"You go ahead. I am feeling under the weather." She sat down in the rocking chair beside my bed.

"But it'll help!" I went over and tugged her arm, realizing it was the one with the long scar of what had been clawed. She winced in pain. "I'm sorry, I'm sorry!"

"It's okay. You won't be alone; you'll be going with Jack. I'll have lunch prepared for you when you get back and if you'd like to invite him along too, you can." She began rocking in the chair and pulled the Bible off my nightstand, flipping through its pages.

If there was one thing I knew about my mother, it was that she was nearly as stubborn as me. Since she already had it in her mind she wasn't coming, there was no way I was going to get her to.

"Suit yourself…but the offer still stands."

She nodded, not looking up but now fixated on one particular page. I rummaged through my armoire and pulled out several dresses; hanging each one back up. The last one I took out was beige and came with matching lace gloves. I quickly slipped it on and placed my hat on my head, remembering that I had been making Jack wait all along. I walked over to Mother real quick and gave her a hug.

"I love you." I rushed out the door.

"I love you too!" she called after me.

As soon as I got downstairs, Jack was looking out the back window.

"Jack, we need to find the beast before it gets to someone," I said.

"When we go to church today, do you think we could warn people there?" he asked.

"We could try…"

It was dead silence on our way to church. Neither Jack nor I even glanced at one another. We braced ourselves for what was to come. It almost felt like the calm before the storm that was about to occur. But there was only one way we could prevent it, and that was to convince everyone not to go to the island.

The church bells sang as the others filed their way in. Many families with young children, but also some widows who, too, lost their husbands to the war just like Mother had. It felt strange going to church without Mother, and I wondered if she was okay. When she was slashed by the beast…something had changed in her. The fragility of life was very evident at that moment. I would thank God for saving her life.

We both kneeled in the back pew and thoughts rushed in from that morning when we were in a much similar spot in the church on the island, except completely alone. I much rather preferred for it to have been that way, but when we were together, it felt like the entire world stopped anyway at times.

After the first and second readings, we all stood to hear the gospel, which would be followed by the homily. The gospels' messages were applicable no matter what the situation, and almost made you feel less alone in a way.

"Then the eleven disciples went to Galilee, to the mountain where Jesus had told them to go. When they saw him, they worshiped him; but some doubted. Then Jesus came to them and said, 'All authority in heaven and on earth has been given to me. Therefore go and make disciples of all nations, baptizing them in the name of the Father and of the Son and of the Holy Spirit, and teaching them to obey everything I have commanded you. And surely I am with you always, to the very end of the age.'"

(Matt 28:16-20)

"The gospel of the Lord," the priest finished reading.

"Praise to you, Lord Jesus Christ," we replied.

Here, Jack and I were trying to figure out a way to convince everyone not to go to the island. I could only imagine what it must have been like for the disciples to spread the word of the Son of God at that time. When people can't see certain things, that doesn't mean it isn't real. There are many things that cannot be seen, but are in existence. There are also many unanswered questions that, until the end of time, will never have a direct answer. The disciples were spreading good news, whereas I would just be talking about the very opposite…a beast.

"I want you to think about the disciples and how they followed Jesus no matter what he had said," the priest slowly paced back and forth amongst the pews.

"Had Jesus shown them any proof that he was the Son of God? Yes, through miracles and prayer. But had he shown them he was directly from heaven? No. These disciples followed out of pure faith and belief. As long as you go through life following your faith and your belief in God, God will be 'with you always, to the very end of the age' as Matthew said in his gospel."

He paused for a moment and seemed to look directly at me.

"I want you to think of this not just with God, but also with anything in your life. If you believe in it, you will find it some way or other. God has incredible ways of working miracles into your life."

I looked over at Jack and felt he was that miracle I had been looking for all along.

Transparent

20

He looked back at me and seemed to enter my soul just by gazing into my eyes. I reached for his hand beside me and intertwined my fingers in his. The gentle, but firm grasp he had on me made me feel safe again. I rubbed my fingertips against his rough, calloused hands. When I looked at his arm, a sleeve was rolled up and a scar shown on his arm. It appeared to be three long marks. It would have matched Mother's perfectly if not for the fact they were much smaller marks and barely left as much as a gashing wound as hers did. He quickly pulled his sleeve back down with his other arm and broke his gaze from me. Instead, looking forward at the priest.

We had already gone up to receive the Eucharist and were now seated again as we waited for the priest's upcoming announcements. This would be the time that we could warn the others about the island.

"I am sure you have all been waiting for this great news; there will be a feast at the Dominican Father's retreat on the fourth of July! Boats will be available to bring you to and from the island for this feast and there will be hot dogs, hamburgers…well it's called a feast for a reason!"

The others laughed. I squeezed Jack's hand harder than I meant to. For some reason, he wasn't getting up to speak out or anything. I took the chance; it was worth it for the people.

"You can't," I said, letting go of Jack's hand and standing up at my pew. Everyone looked over at me as my voice seemed to echo in the church.

"Excuse me?" one of them said.

I walked forward by the priest and tried to think on a whim of what I could say because I knew that I certainly couldn't tell them there was a beast that lurked on the island.

"You can't stay after dusk; the sandbar will be barely visible, and it can be dangerous out there," I said, knowing that didn't guarantee them not to go to the island. It would at least stop them from being out there when the beast wandered during the night.

The crowd just laughed. I could feel my cheeks as they grew hotter by the moment. Slowly, I sat down and wished I hadn't even said anything at all.

"Yes, make sure you make it home in time for your bedtime!" The priest mocked what I had said. "Thanks, Lucy."

I sank down even farther than I thought I could go. Jack grabbed my hand and squeezed it. When I glanced his way, his eyes looked so sincere. I knew the townspeople would definitely be talking if they hadn't already about Jack and I being together. Coming from a small town, the people grew bored quite easily and had nothing better to talk about. Everyone began clearing out, but we remained there.

"Well, I tried..." I said.

"That's all that matters and maybe they will listen and head out before sunset," he reassured me.

"I know. Now we're going to have to make sure we go to this so we can clear all the people out…"

"I will be by your side every step of the way." He took my hand and kissed my knuckles with ease.

"Jack," I whispered, surprised. When I looked left and right, it didn't seem like anyone saw.

"Did I do something wrong?"

"No, not at all," I admitted. I did like it…more than I probably should have. And I yearned to feel his lips against mine.

"You two don't want us to have the feast, huh?" The priest had walked over to us and by then, there was no one else in the church.

"Well, we just want everyone to be safe," Jack answered before I could. He stood up to face the priest, taking me along with him.

"Are you guys coming?" he asked, looking at Jack, then me, and back to Jack again.

"Yes, we will be coming together."

"See you both there, then!" the priest said, and with that, Jack and I walked out, realizing what we had to do.

Temptation

21

"No temptation has overtaken you except what is common to mankind. And God is faithful; he will not let you be tempted beyond what you can bear. But when you are tempted, he will also provide a way out so that you can endure it."

(Corinthians 10:13)

We were just a few days from the feast. Jack and I had figured out a plan of ensuring that boaters could bring people to and from the island only before sundown that way, it would get the majority of the people off the island. Unfortunately, there would be a few lingering people that would likely stay. Despite the horrors of the beast at night, I found the thought of Jack comforting, to the point I wasn't as scared any longer. But I stayed with Mother in her room every night. At times, I would hear the branches as the wind pushed them into the window and it reminded me of the beast.

The morning before the feast day, I opened Father's journal again...flipping through, looking for anything at all about the beast. It appeared he called it "monster" instead, though.

July 1, 1917

The monster comes at night. He stays dormant on the island until nightfall and that is when he lurks. The one thing he preys on most is the vulnerability of love and heartbreak. The town has been keeping things quiet, but there have been several disappearances of widowed women, along with some men that had been drunk at the bar one second and then missing the next. There was one night I had even seen one wandering out of the bar and down that rocky path. What could I do? What could I say? It almost seemed as though the man was in a trance. He was looking forward, eyes dazed and not a clue as to what was going on in the world around him. At first, I had thought the monster was contained on the island, but Lucy has begun having nightmares of it. She has never even stepped foot on the island. I have made sure of it. She wakes up screaming, saying that its claws are going to kill her. A monster that you cannot escape from even in your own home is the most dangerous one there could ever be. For even when you close your eyes to rest, it is still there...lurking; haunting.

I could feel the goosebumps creep up my arm. For some reason, I didn't remember the nightmares when I was young. I would have to ask Mother about it. Speaking of Mother, she still had not yet come to bed, and it was past the hour. I lit a candle and headed downstairs, pulling up the edge of my nightgown so as to not trip.

When I reached the bottom step, I could see Mother at the back door, also in her nightgown. A draft was let in by the door that was wide open. The chill from the cool air crawled down my back and made me shake.

"Mother?" I asked.

She stayed put, not even flinching in the slightest. I began walking toward her and just then, she walked out the door without even closing it behind her. I followed her and closed the distance between us, grabbing her arm gently this time.

"Let me," was all she said, pulling her arm back and continuing on.

"Let you what?!" I jumped in front of her, attempting to stop her from going any farther. Her gaze was beyond me and she looked as though she was focusing on something. I looked back and realized exactly what it was.

"That's not him."

"He has come back. He wants me to go with him," she said. "Let me go."

I looked back at 'Father' again as he stood with his full military uniform on. Despite the temptation, this time…I knew. It couldn't be him. The denial that I had been in for a decade or so quickly faded into acceptance of the truth. And that truth was that he was gone…in the physical form, anyway. His spirit would always be here, but he was gone. This thing that stood before us closely resembled the devil in its many tempting ways. Like the snake that had tricked Eve into eating the fruit. Or the evil that overcame Cain when he killed his brother, Abel. I wanted so badly to give in to the temptations. If only I could just let myself believe Father was truly back…that it was really him. If only it could have truly been him.

I planted both my feet firmly on the ground and grabbed Mother by each wrist.

"That is not Father. Father would not want you coming out here in your nightgown walking out to the island. He would have come into our home with us, and we would all be sleeping by now. He would have come right up to you and hugged you right away—"

I turned her around so she was no longer facing the ghost and hugged her tightly to me.

"Trust me," I said, looking at the thing that resembled Father so closely. A tear streamed down my cheek, and I felt a pit in my stomach. "I want, more than anything, to see Father again. I want to hug him. I want to not ever let go. I want us to be a family again. I want that to be Father. But the truth is…it isn't. It is something that is trying to lure us to the island. Something that is trying to kill us."

And with that, a frown formed on 'Father's' face and he gradually faded into the air around him until no one was even standing there any longer. Completely leaving, as if he had never been there to begin with. But I now knew he would always remain in my heart. And there, I would keep him safe.

Steady

22

"If I have all faith so as to remove mountains, but I do not have love, I am nothing."

(1 Corinthians 13:2)

The day had finally come for the feast. I was set to meet with Jack and soon, he'd be at my door so we could go together. Ever since that night with Mother and Father's ghost, it seemed to be the elephant in the room. Neither she nor I mentioned it. In fact, we acted as if it hadn't even happened.

"What will you wear today?" She came into my room as I was looking through my wardrobe, knowing full well what I already wanted to wear. I held up the green dress with white polka dots.

"That's your go-to one, huh?"

"I just really like it." I smiled, slipping my nightgown off and pulling the dress over my head.

"You're just like your father. When you find something you like, you don't stray far from it." She walked over to me and started playing with my hair. It made me feel like a young girl again, when I'd just bathed, and she'd make a braid in my hair.

"Do you want to come today?" I asked.

"That's alright; you go on without me. You're going with that fellow, Jack?"

"I'm planning to! He's going to be here any minute."

"Is James going with that girl friend of his, too? You guys oughta double date."

"Mother, what makes you so interested in my love life all of a sudden!?"

"It's just about time you found someone!"

"Well, it's been slim pickings to say the least." I winced when she pulled out a knot in my hair.

"I hope this one works out for you, dear." She let go of my hair and handed me a fedora. "You'll just have to wear this to tame those messy bed curls of yours."

"Gee thanks." I snatched it from her and placed it on my head, walking over to the mirror and realizing she was right.

A knock came at the door. We both jumped, startled and not realizing how much time had passed. I grabbed my bag and started down the stairs. Finally, my leg had healed enough to the point I didn't limp much anymore. When I opened the door, there he stood. I couldn't help but look him up and down; he wore a beige button-down shirt, dark brown dress pants and suspenders that seemed to wrap around his shoulders and back perfectly showing just how slim he was.

"Well, hello there, pretty lady." He looked me up and down as well.

"You two make a nice couple!" Mother came up from behind me. I could feel my face get red with embarrassment. We hadn't even labeled what we were exactly. So, 'couple' was the first time we had used that line.

"Hello, it's a pleasure!" Jack reached in and shook Mother's small hand. "I will take good care of your daughter."

"Thank you, you better! It is very nice to meet you too. I have heard good things!" She glanced my way, and I only felt my cheeks grow even hotter. Mother had a way of embarrassing me and I knew I had to get Jack out of there soon before she started to share stories of my childhood.

"I'll see you later!" I called out. "Save some iced tea for me!"

"Will do!"

And with that, Jack and I walked down the pathway to the road that led right to the beach.

"Your mother is a nice lady." He looked over at me with those puppy dog eyes that made me want to just fall into his arms. "So, we're a couple, huh?"

"I don't know, are we?" I asked. I wasn't exactly one to have much experience with this, so I wasn't sure what exactly made people an official couple. We had made it to the opening in the bushes and they stood as walls to our left and right. It felt like we were in a whole other world at that moment.

"Would you like to be?" He got in front of me and stopped, taking both of my hands in his.

"I'd very much like it, Jack."

"Well then, will you go steady with me, Lucy?"

"Absolutely," I answered. He held on to my left hand, but released the right and gently touched his palm to my cheek. In the next moment, I felt his lips pressed into mine.

"Is that okay?" he asked, worry in his eyes.

I placed my hand behind his head and pulled him back toward me, kissing him back again and again. I felt my heart race in my chest; I wanted to be even closer to him somehow than I already was. I felt his hand on the small of my back as he continued to press his lips into me again and again.

When I finally pulled away, I felt like I had run a marathon and was out of breath.

"More than okay." I smiled like a young schoolgirl, giddy and full of excitement.

"Good, because I've been dying to do this." He pulled me back into his arms and we continued kissing right there, concealed by the bushes. He gently bit my bottom lip, and I let out a gasp. He seemed to like the sound I made and did it again.

I pulled away to catch my breath.

"Lucy, I am yours," Jack said with a smile. "I don't want anyone else…no matter how hard I have tried to stay away from you, I just want you."

"I wouldn't have it any other way."

The Feast

23

In the same way, after the supper he took the cup, saying, "This cup is the new covenant in my blood, which is poured out for you."

(Corinthians 11:25)

We decided to take the boat ride to the island because it had been high tide. Although it was a short ride, I was already beginning to feel seasick just a few minutes in. When we finally arrived at the dock that had been rebuilt just for the monastery, Jack held out his hand to help me off and I leaped over toward him, nearly falling into his arms. If he hadn't been so balanced, I was afraid I'd surely knock both of us down and into the water.

"I've got you," he reminded me.

I looked back into his eyes and smiled. It had been a very long time since I had that feeling. Nearly most of my life, I had been the one looking after others and taking care of what was left of my family. I wasn't sure if I would ever get used to being taken care of, but it was very nice.

We walked down the dock, and I felt my feet sink into the sand with the very first step I took off the boat. The smell of hot dogs and hamburgers filled the air in an aroma that reminded me of summertime-get-togethers way back when. As we followed our noses, Jack and I agreed to split up and pass on the word about getting out before sunset. We agreed upon meeting up again at the church that we had been in just a few days prior.

"Lucy!!" James yelled out, and I jerked back around, finding he was just getting out of another boat at a nearby dock with his lady friend, Amy. When I looked back, Jack was already gone into the crowds of people that had arrived with us.

"I didn't know you guys were coming!" I said, holding my arms out wide to give Amy a hug and then James.

"Aren't you with Jack?" James asked right away.

"He went on to go grab some food for me. We're going to meet up in a little bit."

"Ah, okay then. Well, why don't you just walk around with us?" Amy asked.

"That's not a bad idea. I am warning everyone to leave before sundown…spread the word if you can."

"We were already planning on it, but what's going on at sundown?" James asked. He had his arm around Amy and the three of us started walking toward the center of the island. We passed by several cabins that mirrored one another in size and color. These were the cabins that Aquinas Retreatants stayed in. Various men would come from Catholic groups as well as many other areas to worship at this retreat. They opened it to the public now and then, but the feast was a celebration that they hoped would draw more attention to it. Part of me wished I, too, could stay on the island if I didn't know of the horrors. However, it was a wonder as to how the men in the cabins were safe and sound. I was pondering it when I realized Amy and James had been speaking to me the entire time and I was simply ignoring them.

"What?" I asked, not hearing a word they said.

"Your mother was right. You do have selective listening!" James declared, proud of himself for remembering that tidbit from long ago. When we were children, Mother was convinced that I was deaf, or at least partially deaf, because I wouldn't listen. The doctor had joked I had 'selective listening,' which is, of course, not a real thing.

"Don't you two lovebirds have somewhere to be?" I asked, knowing full well James was going to turn bright red from that comment. I could tell he was mustering up the strength not to find any other snarky responses to hit me right back with.

"What were you thinking about?" James changed the subject. *My 'little brother' is finally growing up!* I thought.

"Have you heard of the beast on the island?"

"Oh, no…I was afraid of this all along. Is it you?" he asked. Amy started laughing so hard I thought she was about to fall over.

"No, you silly. Okay, hypothetically speaking…if there were a beast on the island, how would all the men who stayed in the cabins here remain safe? But then some die like those men on the boat that capsized?"

Just then, someone came up from behind me and I saw James and Amy's faces become much more serious than they had just been.

"There are rumors of this said 'beast,' but hypothetically speaking…the beast would not be allowed on holy grounds. That is why the men are safe where they are," the Dominican priest said. He had started the Aquinas Retreat.

"Father Edmund A. Baxter." He held out his hand, and I took it in mine, shaking it.

"I know you," he said.

"Me?"

"Come walk awhile. I'll tell you everything there is to know about this place." He guided me in another direction, and I looked over at James and Amy as they waved goodbye. My part of the plan with Jack had completely gone null and void, as I was now on a 'tour' with the priest that I had no choice but to go with. It was his whole idea for the retreat, anyway.

Four

24

"Whether you turn to the right or to the left, your ears will hear a voice behind you, saying, 'This is the way; walk in it.'"

(Isaiah 30:21)

"How do you know me?" I asked. I felt like I hadn't seen him before and Lord knows how many people he ran into, but for some reason, I stood out to him.

"I knew your father. I was a chaplain in the war. I helped your mother get through difficult times. She has told me a lot about you," he said.

"What did you know about my father?" I asked, curiosity piqued.

"I know he would have done anything for his family, of course. He was one to not even hesitate if it meant keeping you and your mother safe. And that is why he frequented the island before he left for the draft."

"You know about his visits here?"

"Certainly," he said. "So, if you walk this way...you will see the grotto." He gestured over to the stone wall built in the shape of a crescent moon around a statue of Our Lady. I traced my fingertips along the stones and despite the summer heat, they were still ice cold to the touch somehow, shocking me. I jumped.

"Do you know why he visited so much?" I asked as he waved his hand to continue following him past the grotto. There was a bench right in front of it that I assumed the many visitors sat on and prayed at.

"Just like you, he believed there to be a beast."

I stopped right in my tracks. What the priest was saying matched up with Father's journal entries almost perfectly. And it brought that much more truth to the horrors that lurked on the island.

"Do you believe there to be one?"

He turned around and gently placed his hands on my shoulders, looking down at me with compassion in his eyes.

"My dear, it is not about what I believe. It is the simple fact that for every good, there is a bad in this world that must balance it out."

I could feel my heart skip a beat. Without directly saying it, he clearly did believe there was a beast on this island. I wondered why he would still bother coming here if there was such a horrible creature lurking around. Or did he believe that was possible anywhere in this world?

"Come on, I've got to finish showing you the rest before they run out of food, and you end up with just buns!" He continued on as if what he said wasn't groundbreaking whatsoever.

I sped up my pace, not really caring much for food at the moment, as I had so many lingering questions I wished I could ask, but knew better than to drown him with them all.

We came up to a high mound of rocks with a statue of St. Christopher at the very top. From what I knew about St. Christopher, he symbolized protection for travelers. I had an idea as to who the statue must have been for, but knew the Father would explain it.

"This is a shrine that has been dedicated to the victims of the boat that capsized." He slowly kneeled and made the sign of the cross, kissing his hand and touching his palm to the stone foundation.

I felt I should follow suit and kneeled too, making the sign of the cross and kissing the stone beside the one that he had.

We continued on and he pointed to a longer building than most of the cabins of which he said was the dining and recreation hall. Moving onward, he pointed at the chapel, which I had already been in with Jack. It was on stilts; I assumed because of the high tide at times. There was a giant cross along the pathway to the chapel, which had been painted white. At the very top of the roof was another cross, much smaller in size. The chapel looked very much like an old schoolhouse.

"I'm going to take you back to the dining and recreation hall, but feel free whenever you'd like…to come to the chapel to pray. It is open for anyone, no matter what."

"Thank you, Father." I felt the need to bow to him for some reason, so I did.

"Lucy," he said.

"Yes, Father?"

"Your father loved you very much. Whether there is a beast that lurks here or not, just know that you will always be safe in the church, no matter what. Any holy grounds, for that matter."

I felt the uncontrollable tears stream down my cheeks.

"I wish he was here, Father. I can't let Mother see my tears like this. I must be strong for her. I am afraid that if I break, she, too, will break."

"Tears aren't weakness. There is great strength shown from tears because it is what you have overcome and are continuing to overcome. Every time you cry and work through your sadness, think of yourself as a flower that is watered each time. You will only grow stronger and stronger."

He wrapped his arms around me and gave me a hug. I saw Jack walking out of the recreation and dining hall with two plates; one with a hot dog on it and the other with a cheeseburger.

"Thank you, Father," I said.

"Just remember your strength and where you come from. Never forget."

All Yours

25

"Therefore what God has joined together, let no one separate."

(Mark 10:9)

There are many people that come into your life and leave almost as quickly. But then others...stay in your life and make a lasting impact forever on your soul. In certain cases, the people who make the biggest impact on you are ones that you never expected. It could have been a stranger that you exchanged 'hellos' with one day, knowing for sure you would never lay eyes on them again, and that was fine. You could have never known they would turn into that special someone who would make your heart yearn for more and more. The moments in which you are apart are some of the most difficult to endure; all you can think about is their presence by your side. It doesn't matter what you are doing with them; you can be in complete and utter silence and still not be bored in the slightest. For even in your time apart, your souls become bonded by a force that feels as great as God.

Like clockwork, Jack seemed to know I was coming back and had a plate of food saved and ready for me. He told me of all the people he had told to leave before sundown, and I just nodded and hoped he wouldn't ask me if I stuck to the plan because there were barely any people that I was able to warn. I decided to show him around the various cabins, shrines and chapel just like the priest had shown me.

"It was comforting when the priest told me the beast would not be able to come out on holy grounds," I said, reassuring myself again that all would somehow be okay.

"That explains a lot!" he said. "So, if there are still people on the island, then we will just have to make sure they stay in the cabins for their own safety."

"They would probably believe us more if we said that there were bear sightings."

"That is a good point, Lucy," he said, sitting down before the grotto. He began praying, quietly.

"Jack?"

"Yes, love?" He made the sign of the cross and stayed where he was, gesturing for me to come over to sit beside him.

"What do you pray for?" I asked.

"I pray to my mother and father. I thank them for the life I have been given. But I feel like I have been praying for someone like you to come along," he said.

"And now that I'm here?"

"I need to keep you."

"That can't be too hard, can it?" I said, leaning closer to him. He finally looked back at me.

"Not for me." He closed the distance between us and pressed his lips on mine. When he pulled away, I pressed into him again, not wanting to stop. It was a feeling as if I couldn't get enough, but I was fully satisfied at the same time somehow. He rested his hand on the small of my back, continuing to kiss me over and over. I could barely catch my breath, but stopping was out of the question.

I moved my lips over his cheek and down his neck, only to hear him gasp.

"Lucy," he said, pulling away and holding each of my hands in his own.

"What, Jack?"

"This is dangerous. So very dangerous."

"How?"

"I am losing control because you have my heart."

"I promise to take care of it if you take care of mine," I replied, pressing my palm against his chest.

"For as long as you'll have me, I promise to always take care of you. In every way; every aspect. No matter what," he said, standing up and grabbing my hand. "Come."

I followed him all the way past the dining and recreation hall, past the chapel and to the cabins. He pulled me into one and it was completely bare of anyone, as they had all still been in the dining and recreation hall. He closed the door behind us and locked it.

"What if someone comes?" I asked, worried, knowing full well what was about to happen.

"They won't, love."

And with that, I pushed him all the way back onto one of the beds, pressing him down. He easily let me control the situation, but in a moment, he effortlessly picked me up and placed me where he had just been lying.

"Jack," I whispered.

"I won't hurt you," he answered my question before I could even ask.

He began kissing down my neck, and I couldn't help but moan. He covered my mouth to stifle more moans and picked up the hem of my dress, folding it over my chest. He continued farther down and I felt like he must have kissed every inch of my body. He took each of my hands in his own and brought his lips back to mine. I felt him slowly press himself into me; my eyes shot open wide. He went even slower as I got used to him and in the next moment, he covered my mouth with his hand and went even faster. I felt a mix of euphoria and pleasure all at once. My head felt as if it was floating up in the clouds somewhere. He stared into my eyes and started going slow again, taking his hand off my mouth and replacing it with his lips instead. I could feel his body jolt in a way as he pulled himself out and lay beside me, gasping.

"You are mine," he whispered, pulling my body close to him so that I was lying in his arms.

"All yours."

Lurking

26

"**F**or if anyone is a hearer of the word and not a doer, he is like a man who looks intently at his natural face in a mirror. For he looks at himself and goes away and at once forgets what he was like. But the one who looks into the perfect law, the law of liberty, and perseveres, being no hearer who forgets but a doer who acts, he will be blessed in his doing."

(James 1:22-25)

We lay like that for what seemed like hours. I was in his arms, warm and safe. Suddenly, there was a chill that crept down my spine and awoke me. I rolled over to find Jack missing. There was just a blanket covering me that he must have placed over me. I jumped out of bed and struggled to get my clothes back on quickly so I could find out where he went. The cabin that we had been in was still completely empty, but even more-so now without him.

When I walked outside, no one was around, and the sun was just going down. I wondered how long I had been asleep. Making my way back to the dining and recreation hall, I could see many people had already cleared out. Upon entering the hall, there were only a few men that remained, and they were cleaning up after the feast.

"Have you seen Jack?" I asked, voice echoing in the almost empty room.

"Who?" one of them asked.

"Never mind, I'll keep looking."

Back outside, I knew my time was running out, but I needed to find him before leaving the island. The boats had already left the docks and guests must have all cleared out while I was sleeping.

"Jack!" I called out, not caring who heard me.

A dark bird with a patch of red on each side of its wings swooped down before me and flew toward the front of the island, down the path back to the mainland that was still visible.

I went the opposite way the bird had gone and continued toward the chapel.

"Lucy," a familiar voice called out. It wasn't Jack's. It was a voice I had heard long ago and yearned for ever since they left.

"Father?" I turned around and saw him. I tried to fight the temptation to go right to him, just like Mother had.

"You don't have to come here, but I want to warn you…" he said, keeping his distance from me.

"Warn me?"

"My dearest Lucy, you know of the beast that lurks on this island that I had tried so very hard to keep you from…be wary of those that you let close to you."

"What do you mean, Father?" I asked, realizing this wasn't just a lure to go straight to the beast. I could tell by the worry in Father's voice that he was sincere, and it was him. I closed the distance between us and went right up to him with my arms out. Without realizing, my embrace went right through him, and I was left hugging my arms to my chest.

"I can't, my dear. But I am always hugging you so close in your heart." Father put out his hand and gently pressed it to my chest, nearly going through me. Even though I couldn't exactly feel his touch, a breeze went straight through me the moment he tried.

"We are lost without you."

"You are not without me. Lucy, leave the island," he warned me again.

I squeezed my eyes, wishing the tears would stop coming down. As soon as I opened them again, Father was gone. The same bird from before, with reddish-orange on its wings, was about a foot away from me, perched on a branch. It appeared to be looking straight at me. Within seconds, it flew toward the mainland just like the previous one had. Was this a sign?

Rain started trickling down from the sky. When I turned, I was closest to the chapel again. I ran in and kneeled in a pew, not knowing where else to look for Jack, but sooner or later, I would have to leave.

"In the name of the Father, the Son and the Holy Spirit. Saint Anthony, please help me find him. I don't want to leave here without him; or the beast may hunt him down and I may never see him again," I prayed to the patron saint of lost things. The rain began to come down much heavier. I ran all the way toward the back of the church where a window had been left open and was letting in rain. As soon as I reached to pull the window in all the way, a monstrous face appeared on the outside with enormous antlers protruding from its head. Its eyes were glowing red and blood dripped from its mouth. I stumbled back, losing my footing completely. From the ground, I could still see the beast, but for some reason it wasn't coming inside the chapel.

The Chapel.

Father Edmund said the beast couldn't enter holy grounds. I was safe here. I hugged my arms close to my chest, staying seated on the floor, afraid to go anywhere else. The beast's antlers struck the sides of the chapel and made an eerie scratching against each and every window as it continuously circled it. And then, the realization struck me. Right now, the beast was hunting me.

I was prey.

The Hunt

27

"So do not fear, for I am with you; do not be dismayed, for I am your God. I will strengthen you and help you; I will uphold you with my righteous right hand."

(Isaiah 41:10)

When you have nothing keeping you safe and are absolutely afraid for your life, there is just one place one can turn to. The many nights that I ached without

Father taught me just how scary life could be like without a protector; someone who was your security blanket in life. A confidant; a person who made life much less alone. Mother had been broken for a long time, just like I had. But now, what I wanted more than to stay alive somehow was to know that Jack was also safe.

I slowly hid between the pews in the chapel, awaiting my demise. I would have to leave at some point, and I felt like I couldn't wait all the way until the next sunrise because nightfall had just come. Wouldn't the beast grow tired and finally leave? Relentless scratching against the windows and sides of the church led me to believe I was going to be there the entire night.

But then it stopped. The silence was deafening to my ears, as it no longer allowed me to know exactly where the beast was. I slowly peeked out of the pew and found no one still.

"Lucy, help!" Jack's voice roared through my ears, breaking the silence.

I got up immediately and peered through the window, finding no one. I crept back toward the front of the church and peered out that window, seeing Jack on his knees, completely helpless. With caution, I slowly opened the front door to the chapel and looked left and right, ensuring the beast had gone.

"Come in here. You'll be safe!" I called out, not wanting to leave.

"I can barely walk. The beast left to the other side of the island; it must have heard something. Help!" he called out.

Looking left and right again, I quickly rushed forward to Jack's side. Just as I was about to put my arm around his back to help lift him up so we could go into the chapel together, my arm went right through him. From the corner of my eye, I could see a smirk on his face and in the next second, he disappeared completely, vanishing into the air as if he had never even been there to begin with.

I tried to sprint back to the chapel so I could stay safe, but it was too late. I felt the wind get knocked out of me as a heavy weight launched itself onto me, pressing me down to the ground. It snarled, showing its sharp fangs that I knew would pierce through my skin at any second. Its red eyes beamed down at me and I tried to scream for help if there was anyone even there, but the pressure it had on my chest stifled any screams I had. It moved its head down to my neck and sank its teeth in. The excruciating pain was something I felt throughout my entire body. At that point, I had accepted I was going to die. All I could think of was my father. I closed my eyes and imagined us again when I was young, and we had gone to the shores to collect seashells. If he were here, he would protect me. He would even give his life. Because he was strong. And he gave that strength to me. I wasn't going to let this beast win. No matter what it took... I would at least go out with a fight. I reopened my eyes and began clawing the beast right back, kicking my legs and shoving, squirming any which way I could.

The beast was being pushed up and off me somehow. When I looked at its shoulders, I could see Father's hands pushing it up.

"Go! Follow the bird," he screamed. I wanted to look back at him. I wanted to be with him. But I couldn't. I ran, sobbing the entire way back to see if the pathway was even visible. Realizing I lost my shoes back when the Wendigo had pinned me down, my feet were sore and probably cut up and bleeding, but I didn't care. Father was strong for me when I needed him to be; so I needed to be strong for him. I needed to make everything he had done and sacrificed in his life worth it.

My feet sank into the sand with each step. The red-winged blackbird was back, soaring right in front of me, gliding around the perimeter of the island for me to follow its lead. I assumed it would bring me to the path. When I looked over my shoulder, I could see the beast running after me. Father must've not been able to hold him down any longer. I had just made it by the pathway, which was completely visible, when I stumbled over a rock and went flying into the water. Before I could regain my standing, I looked in the water's reflection from the moonlight and found Jack's reflection staring back at me.

"Jack?" I asked, turning completely around to find the beast again. But this time…it was different. Its eyes were no longer red. They were now green.

It whimpered, crawling over to the water. I followed its gaze. Just past the Wendigo's thick fur was its reflection.

And in its reflection was not a beast in the slightest…oh, it was not even a monster.

It was Jack.

The Truth

28

ove does not delight in evil but rejoices with the truth."

(Corinthians 13:6)

What had once been a pure sight of evil faded as the beast's fur withered away and its body slimmed down, taking the antlers in and all and becoming what it once was again…human. Jack lay there on his side, marked up all over his body from my relentless scratching and kicking earlier. I felt the wound on my neck that had just stopped bleeding; looking down, my dress was completely ripped up and stained with blood. I wasn't sure if it was his or my own. As angry as I was at the damage he had done, I felt like I was looking at someone else. In my heart, the Wendigo was not truly Jack. I couldn't get myself to leave him there, laying on his side.

"You need…" he gasped, awakening, and I nearly jumped back. "You need to get as far as you can from me." He turned his head away from me, clearly not wanting to face me in the slightest way.

"Jack." I felt my heart sink, not knowing what to do.

"Run."

I got up and walked over to the other side, where he had turned so he couldn't face me any longer. His eyes were open, and I gently placed my hand down on his shoulder where most of the marks had been. He winced at the pain.

"I'm not afraid," I assured him.

"You should be." He got up, and I gave him a shawl that had been wrapped around my waist so he could cover himself with it. He lost all the clothes he had been wearing when he turned into the beast.

"You could have killed me, but you didn't."

"The bar is set really high for you, huh?" he muttered.

"How long did you know?" I asked.

"Know what?" Jack sat up, still looking down and attempting to keep his distance from me.

"That you are the Wendigo."

"Lucy…stay away from me. For your own good. You heard your father, watch out for those who you keep close to you." He slowly got up, giving me the shawl back and walked away from the pathway.

I looked over to my right and saw the red-winged blackbird flying toward the pathway again and then back to me as if it was pacing.

"I know I should, but I don't want to. We can't let fear win."

I turned the other way and sped up my pace to catch up with Jack, who was still, thankfully, Jack. He continued walking, ignoring the fact I was following him, and we went all the way to the very back edge of the island. He entered a small cave. At first, I crossed my arms and absolutely did not want to enter. What if he turned back into the Wendigo? I was crazy for following him this far, but for some reason, I felt I could trust him. Somehow, I got him to stop. Father did, but then what about at the waters...as soon as he saw his reflection, the truth seemed to set him free.

"I'm coming in," I called out as I entered the cave, too. There was not much inside, and it was very small, but he was already fully clothed again and on his way back out of the cave.

"Okay, I guess not," I said, turning around to leave it as well. He must have kept clothes there. I followed him back to the sandy shore, where he sat on a flat rock. I sat down beside him and watched as he skipped rocks. There was a pile beside him that I feared would topple down at any second. I carefully took one in my hand and skipped it four times. He looked over, impressed, but misery washed over his face almost instantly.

"How can you still be here?" he asked.

"As I said, if you really wanted to hurt me, then you would have…"

He turned, touching my neck gently. I squeezed my eyes in pain just at the touch.

"This, Lucy. This. You should never be harmed in any way. But I did this. I hurt you. It was me."

"Don't you see? It wasn't you, Jack."

"Then who was it?"

"The Wendigo."

"That is me."

"I refuse to believe that." I stood up and placed my hands on his shoulders. "If you could have helped it, you would have."

"Lucy, those marks are only a small fraction of what I am capable of doing to you. I could rip your limbs straight off your body without barely even trying. You asked me how long I knew about this…for a while, but I thought this curse was done because I hadn't woken up here in a while. But then…"

"You came over and saw the marks on the window."

"Yes," he sighed. "That's why I didn't talk to you for a while after that. I realized the curse was trying to lure you to the island…to me…and I don't want to kill you."

"But you didn't."

"I didn't. I don't know what got me to stop, but I don't want to put you in that position again."

"You saw your reflection in the water and remembered who you were. That's when you were Jack again."

"How do you know?" he asked.

"Because I saw it right in front of my eyes."

"Lucy..."

"Jack, you can think I am crazy all you want, but I don't want to be apart from you."

"You need to be for your own good, though." He stood up and took my hands in his own. "I would rather you be safe and not in my life than to put you at risk again."

"I trust you," I said.

"I don't think you know the extent of this curse. My whole life...I had been adopted; I said I had...but the truth is that I was an orphan my entire life. I taught myself everything I know. And when this started happening...I had just turned eighteen. It never happened when I was a child."

"How did you find out it was a curse?"

"I visited the local tribe when I found who my ancestors were. I had been left with just a small backpack when I was young and in that, I found an old photograph. When I brought it to the tribe, they told me about the curse."

"And what did they say?"

"Every man from the lineage of the chief...Catori will turn into the Wendigo at nightfall," he said. "There is nothing I can do to control it."

"We just did," I reminded him.

"I don't want to risk it, but here you are...a defenseless lamb staring a wolf directly in the eyes."

"And so the wolf fell for the lamb..." I looked into his green eyes, accepting my fate.

Wolf & Lamb

29

"The wolf shall dwell with the lamb."
(Isaiah 11:6)

There were some things in life we knew were not good for us. But for whatever reason, we continued to pursue them no matter what the cost. In a way, it was like playing with fire. However many times you got burned, you didn't stop enjoying the flames that danced before your eyes.

It had been months since I found out the truth about Jack. However, there were no more deaths. In the cave on the island, we made sure to fill it with mirrors so Jack could see his true self. The key was remembering who he was. As long as he did so, he could change back on his own. We went back to the island many times together; I had always been looking for Father again but he was nowhere to be found.

When the moon was at its fullest in the sky, casting light upon the island, I walked beside Jack because he said we had to discuss something important. I was almost wondering if he had found my father, and I could finally see him again.

"Why did we have to come out tonight? It's cold and nearly winter." I hugged my chest, keeping my hands in my sleeves for warmth. Jack wrapped his arm around me as we strolled along the sandy shores.

"Can you sit on that rock right there?" he asked.

"Is this a joke?" I pressed my feet firmly on the ground, ready to just turn back. We had come all this way to sit on a rock.

"Come on, just humor me… please?" he persisted.

"Okay, okay!" I walked over to the rock and just as I was about to sit down, a faint blueish glow came from the trees within the forest of the island.

"Why did you stop?" Jack broke the silence.

"Shhh!" I didn't even want to blink for a second, fearing I would lose sight of whatever it was. I walked past the rock and felt a cool breeze rush through me. As I grew closer, I saw exactly what it was and ran as fast as I could toward it.

"Father!" I screamed, delighted. I could hear the leaves crunch behind me as Jack followed. Before my eyes, Father was in his military uniform just as I would usually see him, but he appeared much different. His face was no longer serious, but instead…he was happy. There were tears coming from his eyes. I wished I could give him a hug more than anything.

"Why are you crying?" I asked, but he was looking at Jack instead of me. "Jack?"

"He knows."

"About what?" I asked, confused. They both seemed to know something I didn't. Father walked over to Jack and pressed his hand against Jack's chest. It looked as though it nearly shocked him.

"You have my blessing," Father told Jack. "I tried to keep her away, but I now realize she was the only answer to the curse all along. She may think that it is those silly mirrors, but in all…it is love. The love you feel has the strength of taming the beast and keeping it at bay. Take care of my baby."

"What is going on here?"

Father looked over at Jack and that seemed to prompt him to do something he had intended all along. Jack got down on one knee and pulled out a ring from his pocket. He took my hand in his and looked at Father, then back at me.

"Lucy…will you marry me?" he asked.

"Jack! Yes, yes I will!" Jack slid the ring on my finger and stood back up, picking me up in his arms and giving me a big hug. He spun me around and I felt that, for once in a very long time, everything was going to be okay.

"Father! Look!" I exclaimed, so happy that he could see. I jumped out of Jack's arms and walked over to Father, seeing that he no longer had a blueish aura around him.

"What happened to you?" I asked.

"Lucy," he replied. "I am free. I am at peace."

"What does that mean? Are you leaving?" I asked, feeling the hill that I was on had now come crumbling down.

"I will never leave you. I will always be here." he touched his hand to my heart. I wrapped my arms around him and could finally feel him hug me back. I squeezed my eyes shut, trying to rid myself of the tears that poured down my cheeks. I hugged him tighter and tighter until I realized I was just hugging myself.

Falling to my knees, I couldn't help but sob, holding my hands to my face. The possibility of seeing Father again was no more, and that filled me with a great emptiness.

"He's here," Jack reminded me. He, too, got down to his knees and lifted me back up by both of my arms. "He lives on in you."

"I know." I slowed my breathing.

"Lucy, I promise you I will take care of you for the rest of your life. You may be the lamb and I may be the wolf, but no harm will ever come to you again. You have set your father free, but you have also freed me."

Acknowledgements

Thank you to those that I have lost for always sending reminders even when you are no longer here physically. I couldn't have done this without you.

Grandma Neenee, you have always listened to me on the phone go on and on about my writing ideas. There were many times that we would laugh at silly events I'd come up with and then decide on meaningful names for characters. I miss you more than you'll ever know; let your spirit continue on.

Nonna Rose, even before I started publishing my books, you always listened to my handwritten stories that I never finished. I'm glad that I was finally able to complete them and couldn't have done it without your support!

Mom, thank you for your support in my writing and helping with book events. I'm not quite sure I could put up a canopy tent on my own that wouldn't collapse on people! Thank you for accepting payment in hugs and food!

Last, but not least thank you to my family and friends for supporting me on my writing journey and always cheering me on. I couldn't do it without you!

Charles Island Disclosure

Charles Island is located in Milford, Connecticut and is a state park. The sandbar (tombolo) between Silver Sands State Park and Charles Island over washes twice daily with tidal flooding which produces dangerous currents and undertow. No one should walk on any portion of the tombolo when it is covered with water.

Attention Hikers!

It is important to know walking all the way to Charles Island is not always possible. Low tides do not always uncover the tombolo completely. See Milford Harbor/Connecticut tide chart for tide details.

<u>NO CROSSING May 1st to September 9th due to natural area preserve for nesting birds!</u>

Turn the page for a sneak peek of
another Tale of Charles Island:

Presence

AVAILABLE NOW

The Island

1

The calm of the waters always lured people in. A salty taste filled the air along with seagulls chattering about for their next meal. The murky blue pushed many different shells and sea creatures about. Tides brought them up to the sandy shores only to send them back out to sea. They judged where you could go. Sometimes, they would be as close as the nearby grass while other times, the sea would reveal its hidden features.

Many people came to enjoy the beach, but all that visited could not miss the sight of the island. From the coastline, it seemed small, but the closer you would get, the vaster it truly became. Travelers and even nearby residents soon learned the ways of the island. If you visited by foot, you had to wait until low tide. At that point, and only then, the rocky causeway to the island appeared through the depths of the water. Seagulls would hover above this path as if they were the gatekeepers to the island. You could walk there, but only during this short time. As soon as the tide came in, the path disappeared.

Several, if not many, visitors ventured out and were unable to make it back to the coast in time because the tide concealed their way back home. They would still try anyway and were quickly met with the harsh rip currents of the sea as it carried them out, unable to call for help or be heard.

However, trips that were planned accordingly went very smoothly as you could discover the beauty that this island did hold. After crossing the path, one would find a variety of creatures and plants. The most abundant were birds that seemed to circle it endlessly. Several birds including herons, egrets and piping plovers called this place their home. There was a thin strip of sandy shore that outlined the island's perimeter and a dense jungle lied within. From afar, the jungle looked bare with just a few trees. A plethora of trees crowded the center although vines became a contagion to them, choking each tree out one by one. As time went on, what once was a dense jungle diminished into less and less. But you could only view it from its exterior. The inside was marked off by fencing that claimed bird habitats resided within.

The island's original name was Poquahaug which meant cleared land, named by the Paugussett tribe. After the Europeans took this land from the Native Americans, the Paugussett cursed it and any buildings ever built upon its soil. All warnings were ignored as a tobacco plantation was built on it in 1657 by Charles Deal, which is where the islands present name comes from – Charles Island.

Despite the many signs of caution, there were still quite a few people who disobeyed these words as their curiosity drew them in anyway. One of whom had been a young photographer that found himself in a daze when it came to the island's hypnotizing grasp.

About the Author

Marissa is the author of a memoir and the Tales of Charles Island series. Marissa mostly writes fictional stories and began by journaling and writing screenplays in elementary school. She spends much of her time with her pets aside from traveling to new places and teaching. Born and raised in Connecticut, she holds New England close to her heart and many of her stories are based in the suburbs of New England.

She has a deep and profound respect for people with special needs as her first job in her field was a special educator. Marissa found her voice through writing. While in high school, she was the editor of the Arts and Entertainment section of the school newspaper. She pursued a degree in Education, minoring in English literature and Anthropology. Later, she went back to school to better understand Autism and graduated with a Master's in Special Education.

Marissa would love to hear from you. Use the links below to connect & hear about upcoming books:

Visit Marissa's Website:

www.mystywrites.com

Instagram:

www.instagram.com/_mysty_writes/

Amazon Page:

www.amazon.com/author/marissadangelo